ARTHUR C. CLARKE

Expedition
to Earth

Eleven Science-Fiction Stories

BALLANTINE BOOKS • NEW YORK

To Walter Gillings
—who must share much of the blame.

The story "Expedition to Earth" appeared in *Amazing Stories* under the title "Encounter in the Dawn," Copyright 1953 by Ziff-Davis Publishing Company; "Second Dawn" appeared in *Science Fiction Quarterly* and " 'If I Forget Thee, Oh, Earth' " appeared in *Future combined with Science Fiction Stories,* both Copyright 1951 by Columbia Publications, Inc.; "Breaking Strain" appeared in *Thrilling Wonder Stories* under the title "Thirty Seconds—Thirty Days," Copyright 1949 by Standard Magazines, Inc.; "History Lesson" appeared in *Startling Stories,* Copyright 1949 by Better Publications, Inc.; "Superiority" appeared in *The Magazine of Fantasy and Science Fiction,* Copyright 1951 by Fantasy House, Inc.; "Loophole," "Inheritance," and "Hide and Seek" appeared in *Astounding Science Fiction,* Copyright 1946, 1948, and 1949 respectively by Street & Smith Publications, Inc.; "Exile of the Eons" appeared in *Super Science,* Copyright 1950 by Popular Publications, Inc.; "The Sentinel" appeared in *The Avon Science Fiction and Fantasy Reader,* Copyright 1951 by Avon Periodicals, Inc.

FIRST PRINTING: DECEMBER 1953
SECOND PRINTING: FEBRUARY 1961
THIRD PRINTING: JULY 1965
FOURTH PRINTING: MARCH 1969

FIRST CANADIAN PRINTING: MARCH 1966

BALLANTINE BOOKS, INC.
101 Fifth Avenue • New York, N. Y. 10003

For the hundreds of thousands of readers who loved *Childhood's End* we present a prime collection of Arthur C. Clarke's science-fiction short stories.

If you read *Childhood's End*, which the *Hartford Times* called "a far more mature piece of writing than most science fiction," you know that Mr. Clarke is a writer of superb talent and genuine intellect. His work is exciting as story and thoroughly stimulating as idea. If you are already a Clarke fan, you will not want to miss this collection. If you have not yet read Clarke, then you have a highly pleasurable discovery awaiting you.

This collection starts with a thrilling short novel about a race of creatures whose minds have far outstripped their bodies' capabilities. And it ends with a beautiful short story that hints at a far universe which has been watching us grow, waiting to contact us as soon as we reach the moon. Between these two stories you will find other sterling examples of the ingenuity of plot, height of imagination, the humor and thoughtfulness that are making Arthur C. Clarke a favorite with a large and rapidly growing audience.

BY ARTHUR C. CLARKE

NON-FICTION

INTERPLANETARY FLIGHT
THE EXPLORATION OF SPACE
THE COAST OF CORAL
THE REEFS OF TAPROBANE
BOY BENEATH THE SEA (with Mike Wilson)
THE FIRST FIVE FATHOMS (with Mike Wilson)
INDIAN OCEAN ADVENTURE (with Mike Wilson)
THE TREASURE OF THE GREAT REEF
    (with Mike Wilson)
THE CHALLENGE OF THE SPACESHIP
THE CHALLENGE OF THE SEA
PROFILES OF THE FUTURE
VOICES FROM THE SKY

FICTION

PRELUDE TO SPACE
THE SANDS OF MARS
AGAINST THE FALL OF NIGHT
ISLANDS IN THE SKY
CHILDHOOD'S END
EXPEDITION TO EARTH
EARTHLIGHT
REACH FOR TOMORROW
THE CITY AND THE STARS
TALES FROM THE "WHITE HART"
THE DEEP RANGE
THE OTHER SIDE OF THE SKY
ACROSS THE SEA OF STARS (Omnibus)
A FALL OF MOONDUST
FROM THE OCEAN, FROM THE STARS (Omnibus)
TALES OF TEN WORLDS
DOLPHIN REEF
GLIDE PATH
PRELUDE TO MARS (Omnibus)
2001: A SPACE ODYSSEY (with Stanley Kubrick)

This is an original novel—not a reprint.

Contents

Second Dawn

"Here they come," said Eris, rising to his forefeet and turning to look down the long valley. For a moment the pain and bitterness had left his thoughts, so that even Jeryl, whose mind was more closely tuned to his than to any other, could scarcely detect it. There was even an undertone of softness that recalled poignantly the Eris she had known in the days before the War—the old Eris who now seemed almost as remote and as lost as if he were lying with all the others out there on the plain.

A dark tide was flowing up the valley, advancing with a curious, hesitant motion, making odd pauses and little bounds forward. It was flanked with gold—the thin line of the Atheleni guards, so terrifyingly few compared with the black mass of the prisoners. But they were enough: indeed, they were only needed to guide that aimless river on its faltering way. Yet at the sight of so many thousands of the enemy, Jeryl found herself trembling and instinctively moved toward her mate, silver pelt resting against gold. Eris gave no sign that he had understood or even noticed the action.

The fear vanished as Jeryl saw how slowly the dark flood was moving forward. She had been told what to expect, but the reality was even worse than she had imagined. As the prisoners came nearer, all the hate and

1

bitterness ebbed from her mind, to be replaced by a sick
compassion. No one of her race need evermore fear the
aimless, idiot horde that was being shepherded through
the pass into the valley it would never leave again.

The guards were doing little more than urge the prisoners on with meaningless but encouraging cries, like
nurses calling to infants too young to sense their thoughts.
Strain as she might, Jeryl could detect no vestige of reason in any of those thousands of minds passing so near at
hand. That brought home to her, more vividly than could
anything else, the magnitude of the victory—and of the
defeat. Her mind was sensitive enough to detect the first
faint thoughts of children, hovering on the verge of consciousness. The defeated enemy had become not even
children, but babies with the bodies of adults.

The tide was passing within a few feet of them now.
For the first time, Jeryl realized how much larger than
her own people the Mithraneans were, and how beautifully the light of the twin suns gleamed on the dark satin
of their bodies. Once a magnificent specimen, towering a
full head above Eris, broke loose from the main body and
came blundering toward them, halting a few paces away.
Then it crouched down like a lost and frightened child,
the splendid head moving uncertainly from side to side
as if seeking it knew not what. For a moment the great,
empty eyes fell full upon Jeryl's face. She was as beautiful, she knew, to the Mithraneans as to her own race—
but there was no flicker of emotion on the blank features,
and no pause in the aimless movement of the questing
head. Then an exasperated guard drove the prisoner back
to his fellows.

"Come away," Jeryl pleaded. "I don't want to see any
more. Why did you ever bring me here?" The last thought
was heavy with reproach.

Eris began to move away over the grassy slopes in
great bounds that she could not hope to match, but as
he went his mind threw its message back to hers. His
thoughts were still gentle, though the pain beneath them
was too deep to be concealed.

"I wanted everyone—even you—to see what we had to

to do to win the War. Then, perhaps, we will have no more in our lifetimes."

He was waiting for her on the brow of the hill, undistressed by the mad violence of his climb. The stream of prisoners was now too far below for them to see the details of its painful progress. Jeryl crouched down beside Eris and began to browse on the sparse vegetation that had been exiled from the fertile valley. She was slowly beginning to recover from the shock.

"But what will happen to them?" she asked presently, still haunted by the memory of that splendid, mindless giant going into a captivity it could never understand.

"They can be taugh how to eat," said Eris. "There is food in the valley for half a year, and then we'll move them on. It will be a heavy strain on our own resources, but we're under a moral obligation—and we've put it in the peace treaty."

"They can never be cured?"

"No. Their minds have been totally destroyed. They'll be like that until they die."

There was a long silence. Jeryl let her gaze wander across the hills, falling in gentle undulations to the edge of the ocean. She could just make out, beyond a gap in the hills, the distant lines of blue that marked the sea— the mysterious, impassable sea. Its blue would soon be deepening into darkness, for the fierce white sun was setting and presently there would only be the red disk— hundreds of times larger but giving far less light—of its pale companion.

"I suppose we had to do it," Jeryl said at last. She was thinking almost to herself, but she let enough of her thoughts escape for Eris to overhear.

"You've seen them," he answered briefly. "They were bigger and stronger than we. Though we outnumbered them, it was a stalemate: in the end, I think they would have won. By doing what we did, we saved thousands from death—or mutilation."

The bitterness came back into his thoughts, and Jeryl dared not look at him. He had screened the depths of his mind, but she knew that he was thinking of the shattered ivory stump upon his forehead. The War had been fought, except at the very end, with two weapons only— the razor-sharp hoofs of the little, almost useless fore-paws, and the unicorn-like horns. With one of these, Eris could never fight again, and from the loss stemmed much of the embittered harshness that sometimes made him hurt even those who loved him.

Eris was waiting for someone, though who it was Jeryl could not guess. She knew better than to interrupt his thoughts while he was in his present mood, and so re-mained silently beside him, her shadow merging with his as it stretched far along the hilltop.

Jeryl and Eris came of a race which, in Nature's lot-tery, had been luckier than most—and yet had missed one of the greatest prizes of all. They had powerful bodies and powerful minds, and they lived in a world which was both temperate and fertile. By human standards, they would have seemed strange but by no means repulsive. Their sleek, fur-covered bodies tapered to a single giant rear-limb that could send them leaping over the ground in thirty-foot bounds. The two forelimbs were much smaller, and served merely for support and steadying. They ended in pointed hoofs that could be deadly in combat, but had no other useful purpose.

Both the Atheleni and their cousins, the Mithraneans, possessed mental powers that had enabled them to de-velop a very advanced mathematics and philosophy: but over the physical world they had no control at all. Houses, tools, clothes—indeed, artifacts of any kind— were utterly unknown to them. To races which possessed hands, tentacles, or other means of manipulation, their culture would have seemed incredibly limited: yet such is the adaptability of the mind, and the power of the commonplace, that they seldom realized their handicaps and could imagine no other way of life. It was natural to wander in great herds over the fertile plains, pausing where food was plentiful and moving on again when it was exhausted. This nomadic life had given them enough leisure for philosophy and even for certain arts. Their telepathic powers had not yet robbed them of their voices and they had developed a complex vocal music and an even more complex choreography. But they took the greatest pride of all in the range of their thoughts: for thousands of generations they had sent their minds roving through the misty infinities of metaphysics. Of *physics*, and indeed of all the sciences of matter, they knew nothing—not even that they existed.

"Someone's coming," said Jeryl suddenly. "Who is it?"

Eris did not bother to look, but there was a sense of strain in his reply.

"It's Aretenon. I agreed to meet him here."

"I'm so glad. You were such good friends once—it upset me when you quarreled."

Eris pawed fretfully at the turf, as he did when he was embarrassed or annoyed.

"I lost my temper with him when he left me during the fifth battle of the Plain. Of course I didn't know then why he had to go."

Jeryl's eyes widened in sudden amazement and understanding.

"You mean—he had something to do with the Madness, and the way the War ended?"

"Yes. There were very few people who knew more about the mind than he did. I don't know what part he played, but it must have been an important one. I don't suppose he'll ever be able to tell us much about it."

Still a considerable distance below them, Aretenon was zigzagging up the hillside in great leaps. A little later he had reached them, and instinctively bent his head to touch horns with Eris in the universal gesture of greeting. Then he stopped, horribly embarrassed, and there was an awkward pause until Jeryl came to the rescue with some conventional remarks.

When Eris spoke, Jeryl was relieved to sense his obvious pleasure at meeting his friend again, for the first time since their angry parting at the height of the War. It had been longer still since her last meeting with Aretenon, and she was surprised to see how much he had changed. He was considerably younger than Eris—but no one would have guessed it now. Some of his once-

golden pelt was turning black with age, and with a flash
of his old humor Eris remarked that soon no one would
be able to tell him from a Mithranean.

Aretenon smiled.

"That would have been useful in the last few weeks.
I've just come through their country, helping to round
up the wanderers. We weren't very popular, as you
might expect. If they'd known who I was, I don't suppose I'd have got back alive—armistice or no armistice."

"You weren't actually in charge of the Madness, were
you?" asked Jeryl, unable to control her curiosity.

She had a momentary impression of thick, defensive
mists forming around Aretenon's mind, shielding all his
thoughts from the outer world. Then the reply came,
curiously muffled, and with a sense of distance that was
very rare in telepathic contact.

"No: I wasn't in supreme charge. But there were only
two others between myself and—the top."

"Of course," said Eris, rather petulantly, "I'm only an
ordinary soldier and don't understand these things. But
I'd like to know just how you did it. Naturally," he added, "neither Jeryl nor myself would talk to anyone
else."

Again that veil seemed to descend over Aretenon's
thoughts. Then it lifted, ever so slightly.

"There's very little I'm allowed to tell. As you know,
Eris, I was always interested in the mind and its work-
ings. Do you remember the games we used to play, when
I tried to uncover your thoughts, and you did your best
to stop me? And how I sometimes made you carry out
acts against your will?"

"I still think," said Eris, "that you couldn't have done
that to a stranger, and that I was really unconsciously
co-operating."

"That was true then—but it isn't any longer. The proof
lies down there in the valley." He gestured toward the
last stragglers who were being rounded up by the guards.
The dark tide had almost passed, and soon the entrance
to the valley would be closed.

"When I grew older," continued Aretenon, "I spent

more and more of my time probing into the ways of the mind, and trying to discover why some of us can share our thoughts so easily, while others can never do so but must remain always isolated and alone, forced to communicate by sounds or gestures. And I became fascinated by those rare minds that are completely deranged, so that those who possess them seem less than children.

"I had to abandon these studies when the War began. Then, as you know, they called for me one day during the fifth battle. Even now, I'm not quite sure who was responsible for that. I was taken to a place a long way from here, where I found a little group of thinkers, many of whom I already knew.

"The plan was simple—and tremendous. From the dawn of our race we've known that two or three minds, linked together, could be used to control another mind, *if it were willing*, in the way that I used to control yours. We've employed this power for healing since ancient times. Now we planned to use it for destruction.

"There were two main difficulties. One was bound up with that curious limitation of our normal telepathic powers—the fact that, except in rare cases, we can only have contact over a distance *with someone we already know*, and can communicate with strangers only when we are actually in their presence.

"The second, and greater problem, was that the massed power of many minds would be needed, and never before had it been possible to link together more than two or three. How we succeeded is our main secret: like all such things, it seems easy now it has been done. And once we had started, it was simpler than we had expected. Two minds are more than twice as powerful as one, and three are much more than thrice as powerful as a single will. The exact mathematical relationship is an interesting one. You know how very rapidly the number of ways a group of objects may be arranged increases with the size of the group? Well, a similar relationship holds in this case.

"So in the end we had our Composite Mind. At first it was unstable, and we could hold it together for only a few seconds. It's still a tremendous strain on our mental resources, and even now we can only do it for—well, for long enough.

"All these experiments, of course, were carried out in great secrecy. If we could do this, so could the Mithraneans, for their minds are as good as ours. We had a number of their prisoners, and we used them as subjects."

For a moment the veil that hid Aretenon's inner thoughts seemed to tremble and dissolve: then he regained control.

"That was the worst part. It was bad enough to send madness into a far land, but it was infinitely worse when you could watch with your own eyes the effects of what you did.

"When we had perfected our technique, we made the first long-distance test. Our victim was someone so well-known to one of our prisoners—whose mind we had taken over—that we could identify him completely and thus the distance between us was no objection. The experiment worked, but of course no one suspected that we were responsible.

"We did not operate again until we were certain that our attack would be so overwhelming that it would end the War. From the minds of our prisoners we had identified about a score of Mithraneans—their friends and kindred—in such detail that we could pick them out and destroy them. As each mind fell beneath our attack, it gave up to us the knowledge of others, and so our power increased. We could have done far more damage than we did, for we took only the males."

"Was that," asked Jeryl bitterly, "so very merciful?"

"Perhaps not: but it should be remembered to our credit. We stopped as soon as the enemy sued for peace, and, as we alone knew what had happened, we went into their country to undo what damage we could. It was little enough."

There was a long silence. The valley was deserted now, and the white sun had set. A cold wind was blowing over the hills, passing, where none could follow it,

out across the empty and untraveled sea. Then Eris
spoke his thoughts almost whispering to Aretenon's
mind.

"You did not come to tell me this, did you? There is
something more." It was a statement rather than a
query.

"Yes," replied Aretenon. "I have a message for you—
one that will surprise you a good deal. It's from Therodimus."

"Therodimus! I thought—"

"You thought he was dead, or worse still, a traitor. He's
neither, although he's lived in enemy territory for the
last twenty years. The Mithraneans treated him as we
did, and gave him everything he needed. They recognized his mind for what it was, and even during the War
no one touched him. Now he wants to see you again."

Whatever emotions Eris was feeling at this news of
his old teacher, he gave no sign of them. Perhaps he was
recalling his youth, remembering now that Therodimus
had played a greater part in the shaping of his mind
than had any other single influence. But his thoughts
were barred to Aretenon and even to Jeryl.

"What's he been doing all this time?" Eris asked at
length. "And why does he want to see me now?"

"It's a long and complicated story," said Aretenon,
"but Therodimus has made a discovery quite as remarkable as ours, and one that may have even greater consequences."

"Discovery? What sort of discovery?"

Aretenon paused, looking thoughtfully along the valley. The guards were returning, leaving behind only the
few who would be needed to deal with any wandering
prisoners.

"You know as much of our history as I do, Eris," he
began. "It took, we believe, something like a million
generations for us to reach our present level of development—and that's a tremendous length of time! Almost
all the progress we've made has been due to our telepathic powers: without them we'd be little different
from all those other animals that show such puzzling re-

semblances to us. We're very proud of our philosophy and
our mathematics, of our music and dancing—but have
you ever thought, Eris, that there might be other lines
of cultural development which we've never even
dreamed of? *That there might be other forces in the
Universe besides mental ones?*"

"I don't know what you mean," said Eris flatly.

"It's hard to explain, and I won't try—except to say
this. Do you realize just how pitiably feeble is our control over the external world, and how useless these limbs
of ours really are? No—you can't, for you won't have
seen what I have. But perhaps this will make you understand."

The pattern of Aretenon's thoughts modulated suddenly into a minor key.

"I remember once coming upon a bank of beautiful
and curiously complicated flowers. I wanted to see what
they were like inside, so I tried to open one, steadying
it between my hoofs and picking it apart with my teeth.
I tried again and again—and failed. In the end, half mad
with rage, I trampled all those flowers into the dirt."

Jeryl could detect the perplexity in Eris's mind, but
she could see that he was interested and curious to know
more.

"I have had that sort of feeling, too," he admitted.
"But what can one do about it? And after all, is it really
important? There are a good many things in this universe
which are not exactly as we should like them."

Aretenon smiled.

"That's true enough. But Therodimus has found out
how to do something about it. Will you come and see
him?"

"It must be a long journey."

"About twenty days from here, and we have to go
across a river."

Jeryl felt Eris give a little shudder. The Atheleni hated
water, for the excellent and sufficient reason that they
were too heavy-boned to swim, and promptly drowned
if they fell into it.

"It's in enemy territory: they won't like me."

"They respect you, and it might be a good idea for you to go—a friendly gesture, as it were."

"But I'm wanted here."

"You can take my word that nothing you do here is as important as the message Therodimus has for you—and for the whole world."

Eris veiled his thoughts for a moment, then uncovered them briefly.

"I'll think about it," he said.

It was surprising how little Aretenon managed to say on the many days of the journey. From time to time Eris would challenge the defenses of his mind with half-playful thrusts, but always they were parried with an effortless skill. About the ultimate weapon that had ended the War he would say nothing, but Eris knew that those who had wielded it had not yet disbanded and were still at their secret hiding place. Yet though he would not talk about the past, Aretenon often spoke of the future, and with the urgent anxiety of one who had helped to shape it and was not sure if he had acted aright. Like many others of his race, he was haunted by what he had done, and the sense of guilt sometimes overwhelmed him. Often he made remarks which puzzled Eris at the time, but which he was to remember more and more vividly in the years ahead.

"We've come to a turning-point in our history, Eris. The powers we've uncovered will soon be shared by the Mithraneans, and another war will mean destruction for us both. All my life I've worked to increase our knowledge of the mind, but now I wonder if I've brought something into the world that is too powerful, and too dangerous, for us to handle. Yet it's too late, now, to re-trace our footsteps: sooner or later our culture was bound to come to this point, and to discover what we have found.

"It's a terrible dilemma: and there's only one solution. We cannot go back, and if we go forward we may meet disaster. So we must change the very nature of our civilization, and break completely with the million generations behind us. You can't imagine how that could be done: nor could I, until I met Therodimus and he told me of his dream.

"The mind is a wonderful thing, Eris—but by itself it is helpless in the universe of matter. We know now how to multiply the power of our brains by an enormous factor: we can solve, perhaps, the great problems of mathematics that have baffled us for ages. But neither our unaided minds, nor the group-mind we've now created, can alter in the slightest the one fact that all through history has brought us and the Mithraneans into conflict—the fact that the food supply is fixed, and our populations are not."

Jeryl would watch them, taking little part in their thoughts, as they argued these matters. Most of their discussions took place while they were browsing, for like all active ruminants they had to spend a considerable part of each day searching for food. Fortunately the land through which they were passing was extremely fertile—indeed, its fertility had been one of the causes of the War. Eris, Jeryl was glad to see, was becoming something of his old self again. The feeling of frustrated bitterness that had filled his mind for so many months had not lifted, but it was no longer as all-pervading as it had been.

They left the open plain on the twenty-second day of their journey. For a long time they had been traveling through Mithranean territory, but those few of their ex-enemies they had seen had been inquisitive rather than hostile. Now the grasslands were coming to an end, and the forest with all its primeval terrors lay ahead.

"Only one carnivore lives in this region," Aretenon reassured them, "and it's no match for the three of us. We'll be past the trees in a day and a night."

"A night—in the forest!" gasped Jeryl, half petrified with terror at the very thought.

Aretenon was obviously a little ashamed of himself.

"I didn't like to mention it before," he apologized, "but there's really no danger. I've done it by myself, several times. After all, none of the great flesh-eaters of

ancient times still exists—and it won't be really dark, even
in the woods. The red sun will still be up."

Jeryl was still trembling slightly. She came of a race
which, for thousands of generations, had lived on the
high hills and the open plains, relying on speed to escape
from danger. The thought of going among trees—and
in the dim red twilight while the primary sun was down
—filled her with panic. And of the three of them, only
Aretenon possessed a horn with which to fight. (It was
nothing like so long or sharp, thought Jeryl, as Eris's had
been.)

She was still not at all happy even when they had spent
a completely uneventful day moving through the woods.
The only animals they saw were tiny, long-tailed creatures that ran up and down the tree-trunks with amazing
speed, gibbering with anger as the intruders passed. It
was entertaining to watch them, but Jeryl did not think
that the forest would be quite so amusing in the night.

Her fears were well founded. When the fierce white
sun passed below the trees, and the crimson shadows of
the red giant lay everywhere, a change seemed to come
over the world. A sudden silence swept across the forest
—a silence abruptly broken by a very distant wail toward which the three of them turned instinctively, an-
cestral warnings shrieking in their minds.

"What was that?" gasped Jeryl.

Aretenon was breathing swiftly, but his reply was
calm enough.

"Never mind," he said. "It was a long way off. I don't
know what it was."

And Jeryl knew that he was lying.

They took turns keeping guard, and the long night
wore slowly away. From time to time Jeryl would awaken
from troubled dreams into the nightmare reality of the
strange, distorted trees gathered threateningly around
her. Once, when she was on guard, she heard the sound
of a heavy body moving through the woods very far
away—but it came no nearer and she did not disturb
the others. So at last the longed-for brilliance of the

white sun began to flood the sky, and the day had come again.

Aretenon, Jeryl thought, was probably more relieved than he pretended to be. He was almost boyish as he frisked around in the morning sunlight, snatching an occasional mouthful of foliage from an overhanging branch.

"We've only half a day to go now," he said cheerfully. "We'll be out of the forest by noon."

There was a mischievous undertone to his thoughts that puzzled Jeryl. It seemed as if Aretenon was keeping still another secret from them, and Jeryl wondered what further obstacles they would have to overcome. By midday she knew, for their way was barred by a great river flowing slowly past them as if in no haste to meet the sea.

Eris looked at it with some annoyance, measuring it with a practiced eye.

"It's much too deep to ford here. We'll have to go a long way upstream before we can cross."

Aretenon smiled.

"On the contrary," he said cheerfully, "we're going *downstream*."

Eris and Jeryl looked at him in amazement.

"Are you mad?" Eris cried.

"You'll soon see. We've not far to go now—you've come all this way, so you might as well trust me for the rest of the journey."

The river slowly widened and deepened. If it had been impassable before, it was doubly so now. Sometimes, Eris knew, one came upon a stream across which a tree had fallen, so that one could walk over on the trunk— though it was a risky thing to do. But this river was the width of many trees, and was growing no narrower.

"We're nearly there," said Aretenon at last. "I recognize the place. Someone should be coming out of those woods at any moment." He gestured with his horn to the trees on the far side of the river, and almost as he did so three figures came bounding out on to the bank. Two of them, Jeryl saw, were Atheleni: the third was a Mithranean.

They were now nearing a great tree, standing by the water's edge, but Jeryl had paid it little attention: she was too interested in the figures on the distant bank, wondering what they were going to do next. So when Eris's amazement exploded like a thunderclap in the depths of her own mind, she was too confused for a moment to realize its cause. Then she turned toward the tree, and saw what Eris had seen.

To some minds and some races, few things could have been more natural or more commonplace than a thick rope tied round a tree trunk, and floating out across the waters of a river to another tree on the far bank. Yet it filled both Jeryl and Eris with the terror of the unknown, and for one awful moment Jeryl thought that a gigantic snake was emerging from the water. Then she saw that it was not alive, but her fear remained. For it was the first artificial object that she had ever seen.

"Don't worry about *what* it is, or how it was put there," counseled Aretenon. "It's going to carry you across, and that's all that matters for the moment. Look—there's someone coming over now!"

One of the figures on the far bank had lowered itself into the water, and was working its way with its fore-limbs along the rope. As it came nearer—it was the Mithranean, and a female—Jeryl saw that it was carrying a second and much smaller rope looped round the upper part of its body.

With the skill of long practice, the stranger made her way across the floating cable, and emerged dripping from the river. She seemed to know Aretenon, but Jeryl could not intercept their thoughts.

"I can go across without any help," said Aretenon, "but I'll show you the easy way."

He slipped the loop over his shoulder and, dropping into the water, hooked his fore-limbs over the fixed cable. A moment later he was being dragged across at a great speed by the two others on the far bank where, after much trepidation, Eris and Jeryl presently joined him.

It was not the sort of bridge one would expect from a race which could quite easily have dealt with the mathe-

matics of a reinforced concrete arch—if the possibility
of such an object had ever occurred to it. But it served
its purpose, and once it had been made, they could use
it readily enough.

Once it had been made. But—who had made it?

When their dripping guides had rejoined them, Aretenon gave his friends a warning.

"I'm afraid you're going to have a good many shocks
while you're here. You'll see some very strange sights,
but when you understand them, they'll cease to puzzle
you in the slightest. In fact, you will soon come to take
them for granted."

One of the strangers, whose thoughts neither Eris nor
Jeryl could intercept, was giving him a message.

"Therodimus is waiting for us," said Aretenon. "He's
very anxious to see you."

"I've been trying to contact him," complained Eris.
"But I've not succeeded."

Aretenon seemed a little troubled .

"You'll find he's changed," he said. "After all, you've
not seen each other for many years. It may be some time
before you can make full contact again."

Their road was a winding one through the forest, and
from time to time curiously narrow paths branched off
in various directions. Therodimus, thought Eris, must
have changed indeed for him to have taken up permanent residence among trees. Presently the track
opened out into a large, semicircular clearing with a low
white cliff lying along its diameter. At the foot of the
cliff were several dark holes of varying sizes—obviously the openings of caves.

It was the first time that either Eris or Jeryl had ever
entered a cave, and they did not greatly look forward
to the experience. They were relieved when Aretenon
told them to wait just outside the opening, and went on
alone toward the puzzling yellow light that glowed in
the depths. A moment later, dim memories began to
pulse in Eris's mind, and he knew that his old teacher
was coming, even though he could no longer fully share
his thoughts.

Something stirred in the gloom, and then Therodimus came out into the sunlight. At the sight of him, Jeryl screamed once and buried her head in Eris's mane, but Eris stood firm, though he was trembling as he had never done before battle. For Therodimus blazed with a magnificence that none of his race had ever known since history began. Around his neck hung a band of glittering objects that caught and refracted the sunlight in myriad colors, while covering his body was a sheet of some thick, many-hued material that rustled softly as he walked. And his horn was no longer the yellow of ivory: some magic had changed it to the most wonderful purple that Jeryl had ever seen.

Therodimus stood motionless for a moment, savoring their amazement to the full. Then his rich laugh echoed in their minds, and he reared up upon his hind limb. The colored garment fell whispering to the ground, and at a toss of his head the glittering necklace arched like a rainbow into a corner of the cave. But the purple horn remained unchanged.

It seemed to Eris that he stood at the brink of a great chasm, with Therodimus beckoning to him on the far side. Their thoughts struggled to form a bridge, but could make no contact. Between them was the gulf of half a lifetime and many battles, of myriad unshared experiences—Therodimus' years in this strange land, his own mating with Jeryl and the memory of their lost children. Though they stood face to face, a few feet only between them, their thoughts could never meet again.

Then Aretenon, with all the power and authority of his unsurpassed skill, did something to his mind that Eris was never quite able to recall. He only knew that the years seemed to have rolled back, that he was once more the eager, anxious pupil—and that he could speak to Therodimus again.

It was strange to sleep underground, but less unpleasant than spending the night amid the unknown terrors of the forest. As she watched the crimson shadows deepening beyond the entrance to the little cave, Jeryl

tried to collect her scattered thoughts. She had understood only a small part of what had passed between Eris
and Therodimus, but she knew that something incredible
was taking place. The evidence of her eyes was enough
to prove that: today she had seen things for which there
were no words in her language.

She had heard things, too. As they had passed one of
the cave-mouths, there had come from it a rhythmic,
"whirring" sound, unlike that made by any animal she
knew. It had continued steadily without pause or break
as long as she could hear it, and even now its unhurried
rhythm had not left her mind. Aretenon, she believed,
had also noticed it, though without any surprise: Eris
had been too engrossed with Therodimus.

The old philosopher had told them very little, pre-
ferring, as he said, to show them his empire when they
had had a good night's rest. Nearly all their talk had
been concerned with the events of their own land during
the last few years, and Jeryl found it somewhat boring.
Only one thing had interested her, and she had eyes for
little else. That was the wonderful chain of colored crystals that Therodimus had worn around his neck. What
it was, or how it had been created, she could not imagine:
but she coveted it. As she fell asleep, she found herself
thinking idly, but more than half seriously, of the sensa-
tion it would cause if she returned to her people with
such a marvel gleaming against her own pelt. It would
look so much better there than upon old Therodimus.

Aretenon and Therodimus met them at the cave soon
after dawn. The philosopher had discarded his regalia—
which he had obviously worn only to impress his guests
—and his horn had returned to its normal yellow. That
was one thing Jeryl thought she could understand, for
she had come across fruits whose juices could cause such
color changes.

Therodimus settled himself at the mouth of the cave.
He began his narration without preliminaries, and Eris
guessed that he must have told it many times before to
earlier visitors.

"I came to this place, Eris, about five years after leav-

ing our country. As you know, I was always interested in
strange lands, and from the Mithraneans I'd heard ru-
mors that intrigued me very much. How I traced them
to their source is a long story that doesn't matter now.
I crossed the river far upstream one summer, when the
water was very low. There's only one place where it can
be done, and then only in the driest years. Higher still
the river loses itself in the mountains, and I don't think
there's any way through them. So this is virtually an
island—almost completely cut off from Mithranean territory.

"It's an island, but it's not uninhabited. The people
who live here are called the Phileni, and they have a
very remarkable culture—one entirely different from our
own. Some of the products of that culture you've already
seen.

"As you know, there are many different races on our
world, and quite a few of them have some sort of intelligence. But there is a great gulf between us and all
other creatures. As far as we know, we are the only beings
capable of abstract thought and complex logical processes.

"The Phileni are a much younger race than ours, and
they are intermediate between us and the other animals.
They've lived here on this rather large island for several
thousand generations—but their rate of development has
been many, many times swifter than ours. They neither
possess nor understand our telepathic powers, but they
have something else which we may well envy—something which is responsible for the whole of their civilization and its incredibly rapid progress."

Therodimus paused, then rose slowly to his feet.

"Follow me," he said. "I'll take you to see the Phileni."

He led them back to the caves from which they had
come the night before, pausing at the entrance from
which Jeryl had heard that strange, rhythmic whirring.
It was clearer and louder now, and she saw Eris start as
though he had noticed it for the first time. Then Therodimus uttered a high-pitched whistle, and at once the
whirring slackened, falling octave by octave until it had

ebbed into silence. A moment later something came toward them out of the semigloom.

It was a little creature, scarcely half their height, and
it did not hop, but walked upon two jointed limbs that
seemed very thin and feeble. Its large spherical head was
dominated by three huge eyes, set far apart and capable
of independent movement. With the best will in the
world, Jeryl did not think it was very attractive.

Then Therodimus uttered another whistle, and the
creature raised its fore-limbs toward them.

"Look closely," said Therodimus, very gently, "and
you will see the answer to many of your questions."

For the first time, Jeryl saw that the creature's fore-
limbs did not end in hoofs, or indeed after the fashion
of any animal with which she was acquainted. Instead,
they divided into at least a dozen thin, flexible tentacles
and two hooked claws.

"Go toward it, Jeryl," commanded Therodimus. "It
has something for you."

Hesitantly, Jeryl moved forward. She noticed that the
creature's body was crossed with bands of some dark
material, to which were attached unidentifiable objects.
It dropped a fore-limb to one of these, and a cover
opened to reveal a cavity, inside which something glittered. Then the little tentacles were clutching that mar-
velous crystal necklace, and with a movement so swift
and dexterous that Jeryl could scarcely follow it, the
Phileni moved forward and clasped it round her neck.

Therodimus brushed aside her confusion and gratitude,
but his shrewd old mind was well pleased. Jeryl would
be his ally now in whatever he planned to do. But Eris's
emotions might not be so easily swayed, and in this
matter mere logic was not enough. His old pupil had
changed so much, had been so deeply wounded by the
past, that Therodimus could not be certain of success.
Yet he had a plan that could turn even these difficulties
to his advantage.

He gave another whistle, and the Phileni made a curious waving gesture with its hands and disappeared into
the cave. A moment later that strange whirring ascended

once more from the silence, but Jeryl's curiosity was now quite overshadowed by her delight in her new possession.

"We'll go through the woods," said Therodimus "to the nearest settlement—it's only a little way from here. The Phileni don't live in the open, as we do. In fact, they differ from us in almost every conceivable way. I'm even afraid," he added ruefully, "that they're much better natured than we are, and I believe that one day they'll be more intelligent. But first of all, let me tell you what I've learned about them, so that you can understand what I'm planning to do."

The mental evolution of any race is conditioned, even dominated, by physical factors which that race almost invariably takes for granted as part of the natural order of things. The wonderfully sensitive hands of the Phileni had enabled them to find by experiment and trial facts which had taken the planet's only other intelligent species a thousand times as long to discover by pure deduction. Quite early in their history, the Phileni had invented simple tools. From these they had proceeded to fabrics, pottery, and the use of fire. When Therodimus had discovered them, they had already invented the lathe and the potter's wheel, and were about to move into their first Metal Age—with all that that implied.

On the purely intellectual plane, their progress had been less rapid. They were clever and skillful, but they had a dislike of abstract thought and their mathematics was purely empirical. They knew, for example, that a triangle with sides in the ratio three-four-five was right-angled, but had not suspected that this was only a special case of a much more general law. Their knowledge was full of such yawning gaps which, despite the help of Therodimus and his several-score disciples, they seemed in no great hurry to fill.

Therodimus they worshipped as a god, and for two whole generations of their short-lived race they had obeyed him in everything, giving him all the products of their skill that he needed, and making at his suggestion the new tools and devices that had occurred to him. The partnership had been incredibly fertile, for it was as if both races had suddenly been released from their shackles. Great manual skill and great intellectual powers had fused in a fruitful union probably unique in all the universe—and progress that would normally have taken millennia had been achieved in less than a decade.

As Aretenon had promised them, though Eris and Jeryl saw many marvels, they came across nothing that they could not understand once they had watched the little Phileni craftsmen at work and had seen with what magic their hands shaped natural materials into lovely or useful forms. Even their tiny towns and primitive farms soon lost their wonder and became part of the accepted order of things.

Therodimus let them look their fill, until they had seen every aspect of this strangely sophisticated Stone Age culture. Because they knew no different, they found nothing incongruous in the sight of a Phileni potter—who could scarcely count beyond ten—shaping a series of complex algebraic surfaces under the guidance of a young Mithranean mathematician. Like all his race, Eris possessed tremendous powers of mental visualization, but he realized how much easier geometry would be if one could actually *see* the shapes one was considering. From this beginning (though he could not guess it) would one day evolve the idea of a written language.

Jeryl was fascinated above all things by the sight of the little Phileni women weaving fabrics upon their primitive looms. She could sit for hours watching the flying shuttles and wishing that she could use them. Once one had seen it done, it seemed so simple and obvious—and so utterly beyond the power of the clumsy, useless limbs of her own people.

They grew very fond of the Phileni, who seemed eager to please and were pathetically proud of all their manual skills. In these new and novel surroundings, meeting fresh wonders every day, Eris seemed to be recovering from some of the scars which the War had left upon his mind. Jeryl knew, however, that there was still much damage to be undone. Sometimes, before he could hide them, she would come across raw, angry wounds in the depths of Eris's mind, and she feared that many of them —like the broken stump of his horn—would never heal. Eris had hated the War, and the manner of its ending still oppressed him. Beyond this, Jeryl knew, he was haunted by the fear that it might come again.

These troubles she often discussed with Therodimus, of whom she had now grown very fond. She still did not fully understand why he had brought them here, or what he and his followers were planning to do. Therodimus was in no hurry to explain his actions, for he wished Jeryl and Eris to draw their own conclusions as far as possible. But at last, five days after their arrival, he called them to his cave.

"You've now seen," he began, "most of the things we have to show you here. You know what the Phileni can do, and perhaps you have thought how much our own lives will be enriched once we can use the products of their skill. That was my first thought when I came here, all those years ago.

"It was an obvious and rather naïve idea, but it led to a much greater one. As I grew to know the Phileni, and found how swiftly their minds had advanced in so short a time, I realized what a fearful disadvantage our own race had always labored under. I began to wonder how much further forward *we* would have been had we the Phileni's control over the physical world. It is not a question of mere convenience, or the ability to make beautiful things like that necklace of yours, Jeryl, but something much more profound. It is the difference between ignorance and knowledge, between weakness and power.

"We have developed our minds, and our minds alone, until we can go no further. As Aretenon has told you, we have now come to a danger that threatens our entire race. We are under the shadow of the irresistible weapon against which there can be no defense.

"The solution is, quite literally, in the hands of the Phileni. We must use their skills to reshape our world,

and so remove the cause of all our wars. We must go back
to the beginning and re-lay the foundations of our culture. It won't be *our* culture alone, though, for we shall
share it with the Phileni. They will be the hands—we
the brains. Oh, I have dreamed of the world that may
come, ages ahead, when even the marvels you see around
you now will be considered childish toys! But not many
are philosophers, and I need an argument more substantial than dreams. That final argument I believe I may
have found, though I cannot yet be certain.

"I have asked you here, Eris, partly because I wanted
to renew our old friendship, and partly because your
word will now have far greater influence than mine. You
are a hero among your own people, and the Mithraneans
also will listen to you. I want you to return, taking with
you some of the Phileni and their products. Show them
to your people, and ask them to send their young men
here to help us with our work."

There was a pause during which Jeryl could gather
no hints of Eris's thoughts. Then he replied hesitantly:

"But I still don't understand. These things that the
Phileni make are very pretty, and some of them may be
useful to us. But how can they change us as profoundly
as you seem to think?"

Therodimus sighed. Eris could not see past the present
into the future that was yet to be. He had not caught, as
Therodimus had done, the promise that lay beyond the
busy hands and tools of the Phileni—the first faint intimations of the Machine. Perhaps he would never understand: but he could still be convinced.

Veiling his deeper thoughts, Therodimus continued:

"Perhaps some of these things are toys, Eris—but they
may be more powerful than you think. Jeryl, I know,
would be loath to part with hers . . . and perhaps I can
find one that would convince you."

Eris was skeptical, and Jeryl could see that he was in
one of his darker moods.

"I doubt it very much," he said.

"Well, I can try." Therodimus gave a whistle, and one

of the Phileni came running up. There was a short ex-
change of conversation.

"Would you come with me, Eris? It will take some
time."

Eris followed him, the others, at Therodimus' request,
remaining behind. They left the large cave and went
toward the row of smaller ones which the Phileni used
for their various trades.

The strange whirring was sounding loudly in Eris's
ears, but for a moment he could not see its cause, the
light of the crude-oil lamps being too faint for his eyes.
Then he made out one of the Phileni bending over a
wooden table upon which something was spinning
rapidly, driven by a belt from a treadle operated by another of the little creatures. He had seen the potters using
a similar device, but this was different. It was shaping
wood, not clay, and the potter's fingers had been replaced
by a sharp metal blade from which long, thin shavings
were curling out in fascinating spirals. With their huge
eyes, the Phileni, who disliked full sunlight, could see
perfectly in the gloom, but it was some time before Eris
could discover just what was happening. Then, suddenly, he understood.

"Aretenon," said Jeryl when the others had left them,
"why should the Phileni do all these things for us? Surely
they're quite happy as they are?"

The question, Aretenon thought, was typical of Jeryl
and would never have been asked by Eris.

"They will do anything that Therodimus says," he answered, "but even apart from that there's so much we
can give them as well. When we turn our minds to their
problems, we can see how to solve them in ways that
would never have occurred to them. They're very eager
to learn, and already we must have advanced their culture by hundreds of generations. Also, they're physically
very feeble. Although we don't possess their dexterity,
our strength makes possible tasks they could never attempt."

They had wandered to the edge of the river, and stood

for a moment watching the unhurried waters moving
down to the sea. Then Jeryl turned to go upstream, but
Aretenon stopped her.

"Therodimus doesn't want us to go that way, yet," he
explained. "It's just another of his little secrets. He never
likes to reveal his plans until they're ready."

Slightly piqued, and distinctly curious, Jeryl obedi-
ently turned back. She would, of course, come this way
again as soon as there was no one else about.

It was very peaceful here in the warm sunlight, among
the pools of heat trapped by the trees. Jeryl had almost
lost her fear of the forest, though she knew she would
never be quite happy there.

Aretenon seemed very abstracted, and Jeryl knew that
he wished to say something and was marshaling his
thoughts. Presently he began to speak, with the freedom
that is possible only between two people who are fond
of each other but have no emotional ties.

"It is very hard, Jeryl," he began, "to turn one's back
on the work of a lifetime. Once I had hoped that the
great new forces we have discovered could be safely
used, but now I know that is impossible, at least for
many ages. Therodimus was right—we can go no further
with our minds alone. Our culture has been hopelessly
one-sided, though through no fault of ours. We cannot
solve the fundamental problem of peace and war without a command over the physical world such as the Phileni possess—and which we hope to borrow from them.

"Perhaps there will be other great adventures here for
our minds, to make us forget what we will have to abandon. We shall be able to learn something from Nature at
last. What is the difference between fire and water, between wood and stone? What are the suns, and what are
those millions of faint lights we see in the sky when both
the suns are down? Perhaps the answers to all these
questions may lie at the end of the new road along which
we must travel."

He paused.

"New knowledge—new wisdom—in realms we have
never dreamed of before. It may lure us away from the

dangers we have encountered: for certainly nothing we
can learn from Nature will ever be as great a threat as
the peril we have uncovered in our own minds."

The flow of Aretenon's thoughts was suddenly interrupted. Then he said: "I think that Eris wants to see you."

Jeryl wondered why Eris had not sent the message to
her: she wondered, too, at the undertone of amusement—
or was it something else?—in Aretenon's mind.

There was no sign of Eris as they approached the caves,
but he was waiting for them and came bounding out into
the sunlight before they could reach the entrance. Then
Jeryl gave an involuntary cry, and retreated a pace or
two as her mate came toward her.

For Eris was whole again. Gone was the shattered
stump on his forehead: it had been replaced by a new,
gleaming horn no less splendid than the one that he had
lost.

In a belated gesture of greeting, Eris touched horns
with Aretenon. Then he was gone into the forest in
great joyous leaps—but not before his mind had met
Jeryl's as it had seldom done since the days before the
War.

"Let him go," said Therodimus softly. "He would
rather be alone. When he returns I think you will find
him—different." He gave a little laugh. "The Phileni are
clever, are they not? Now, perhaps, Eris will be more
appreciative of their 'toys.'"

"I know I am impatient," said Therodimus, "but I am
old now, and I want to see the changes begin in my own
lifetime. That is why I am starting so many schemes in
the hope that some at least will succeed. But this is the
one, above all, in which I have put most faith."

For a moment he lost himself in his thoughts. Not one
in a hundred of his own race could fully share his dream.
Even Eris, though he now believed in it, did so with his
heart rather than his mind. Perhaps Aretenon—the brilliant and subtle Aretenon, so desperately anxious to neu-
tralize the powers he had brought into the world—might

have glimpsed the reality. But his was of all minds the
most impenetrable, save when he wished otherwise.

"You know as well as I do," continued Therodimus, as
they walked upstream, "that our wars have only one
cause—Food. We and the Mithraneans are trapped on
this continent of ours with its limited resources, which
we can do nothing to increase. Ahead of us we have always the nightmare of starvation, and for all our vaunted
intelligence there has been nothing we can do about it.
Oh yes, we have scraped some laborious irrigation ditches
with our fore-hoofs, but how slight their help has been!

"The Phileni have discovered how to grow crops that
increase the fertility of the ground many-fold. I believe
that we can do the same—once we have adapted their
tools for our own use. That is our first and most important
task, but it is not the one on which I have set my heart.
The final solution to our problem, Eris, *must be the discovery of new, virgin lands into which our people can
migrate.*"

He smiled at the other's amazement.

"No, don't think I'm mad. Such lands do exist, I'm sure
of it. Once I stood at the edge of the ocean and watched
a great flight of birds coming inland from far out at sea.
I have seen them flying outward, too, so purposefully
that I was certain they were going to some other country.
And I have followed them with my thoughts."

"Even if your theory is true, which it probably is," said
Eris, "what use is it to us?" He gestured to the river flowing beside them. "We drown in the water, and you cannot build a rope to support us—" His thoughts suddenly
faded out into a jumbled chaos of ideas.

Therodimus smiled.

"So you have guessed what I hope to do. Well, now
you can see if you are right."

They had come to a level stretch of bank, upon which
a group of Phileni were busily at work, under the super-
vision of some of Therodimus' assistants. Lying at the
water's edge was a strange object which, Eris realized,
was made of many tree-trunks joined together by ropes.

They watched in fascination as the orderly tumult

reached its climax. There was a great pulling and push-
ing, and the raft moved ponderously into the water with
a mighty splash. The spray had scarcely ceased to fall
when a young Mithranean leaped from the bank and began to dance gleefully upon the logs, which were now
tugging at the moorings as if eager to break away and
follow the river down to the sea. A moment later he had
been joined by others, rejoicing in their mastery of a new
element. The little Phileni, unable to make the leap,
stood watching patiently on the bank while their masters
enjoyed themselves.

There was an exhilaration about the scene that no one
could miss, though perhaps few of those present realized that they were at a turning point in history. Only
Therodimus stood a little apart from the rest, lost in his
own thoughts. This primitive raft, he knew, was merely
a beginning. It must be tested upon the river, then along
the shores of the ocean. The work would take years, and
he was never likely to see the first voyagers returning
from those fabulous lands whose existence was still no
more than a guess. But what had been begun, others
would finish.

Overhead, a flight of birds was passing across the
forest. Therodimus watched them go, envying their freedom to move at will over land and sea. He had begun the
conquest of the water for his race, but that the skies
might one day be theirs also was beyond even his imagination.

Aretenon, Jeryl, and the rest of the expedition had already crossed the river when Eris said good-bye to Therodimus. This time they had crossed without a drop of
water touching their bodies, for the raft had come downstream and was performing valuable duties as a ferry.
A new and much improved model was already under
construction, as it was painfully obvious that the proto-
type was not exactly seaworthy. These initial difficulties
would be quickly overcome by designers who, even if
they were forced to work with Stone Age tools, could

handle with ease the mathematics of metacenters, buoy-
ancies, and advanced hydrodynamics.

"Your task won't be a simple one," said Therodimus,
"for you cannot show your people all the things you have
seen here. At first you must be content to sow the seed,
to arouse interest and curiosity—particularly among the
young, who will come here to learn more. Perhaps you
will meet opposition: I expect so. But every time you
return to us, we shall have new things to show you to
strengthen your arguments."

They touched horns: then Eris was gone, taking with
him the knowledge that was to change the world—so
slowly at first, then ever more swiftly. Once the barriers
were down, once the Mithraneans and the Atheleni had
been given the simple tools which they could fasten to
their fore-limbs and use unaided, progress would be
swift. But for the present they must rely on the Phileni
for everything: and there were so few of them.

Therodimus was well content. Only in one respect was
he disappointed, for he had hoped that Eris, who had
always been his favorite, might also be his successor.
The Eris who was now returning to his own people was no
longer self-obsessed or embittered, for he had a mission
and hope for the future. But he lacked the keen, far-
ranging vision that was needed here: it would be Aretenon who must continue what he had begun. Still, that
could not be helped, and there was no need yet to think
of such matters. Therodimus was very old, but he knew
that he would be meeting Eris many times again here by
the river at the entrance to his land.

The ferry was gone now, and though he had expected
it, Eris stopped amazed at the great span of the bridge,
swaying slightly in the breeze. Its execution did not quite
match its design—a good deal of mathematics had gone
into its parabolic suspension—but it was still the first
great engineering feat in history. Constructed entirely
of wood and rope though it was, it forecast the shape of
the metal giants to come.

Eris paused in the middle. He could see smoke rising

from the shipyards facing the ocean, and thought he
could just glimpse the masts of some of the new vessels
that were being built for coastal trade. It was hard to
believe that when he had first crossed this river he had
been dragged over, dangling from a rope.

Aretenon was waiting for them on the far bank. He
moved rather slowly now, but his eyes were still bright
with the old, eager intelligence. He greeted Eris warmly.

"I'm glad you could come now. You're just in time."

That, Eris knew, could mean only one thing.

"The ships are back?"

"Almost: they were sighted an hour ago, out on the
horizon. They should be here at any moment, and then
we shall know the truth at last, after all these years. If
only—"

His thoughts faded out, but Eris could continue them.
They had come to the great pyramid of stones beneath
which Therodimus lay—Therodimus, whose brain was
behind everything they saw, but who could never learn
now if his most cherished dream was true or not.

There was a storm coming up from the ocean, and
they hurried along the new road that skirted the river's
edge. Small boats of a kind that Eris had not seen before
went past them occasionally, operated by Atheleni or
Mithraneans with wooden paddles strapped to their fore-
limbs. It always gave Eris great pleasure to see such new
conquests, such new liberations of his people from their
age-old chains. Yet sometimes they reminded him of
children who had suddenly been let loose into a wonderful new world, full of exciting and interesting things that
must be done, whether they were likely to be useful or
not. However, anything that promised to make his race
into better sailors was more than useful. In the last decade Eris had discovered that pure intelligence was sometimes not enough: there were skills that could not be
acquired by any amount of mental effort. Though his
people had largely overcome their fear of water, they
were still quite incompetent on the ocean, and the Phileni
had therefore become the first navigators of the world.

Jeryl looked nervously around her as the first peal of

thunder came rolling in from the sea. She was still wearing the necklace that Therodimus had given her so long ago: but it was by no means the only ornament she carried now.

"I hope the ships will be safe," she said anxiously.

"There's not much wind, and they will have ridden out much worse storms than this," Aretenon reassured her, as they entered his cave. Eris and Jeryl looked round with eager interest to see what new wonders the Phileni had made during their absence: but if there were any they had been hidden away, as usual, until Aretenon was ready to show them. He was still rather childishly fond of such little surprises and mysteries.

There was an air of absent-mindedness about the meeting that would have puzzled an onlooker ignorant of its cause. As Eris talked of all the changes in the outer world, of the success of the new Phileni settlements, and of the steady growth of agriculture among his people, Aretenon listened with only half his mind. His thoughts, and those of his friends, were far out at sea, meeting the on-coming ships, which might be bringing the greatest news their world had ever received.

As Eris finished his report, Aretenon rose to his feet and began to move restlessly around the chamber.

"You have done better than we dared to hope at the beginning. At least there has been no war for a generation, and our food supply is ahead of the population for the first time in history—thanks to our new agricultural techniques."

Aretenon glanced at the furnishings of his chamber, recalling with an effort the fact that in his own youth almost everything he saw would have appeared impossible or even meaningless to him. Not even the simplest of tools had existed then, at least in the knowledge of his people. Now there were ships and bridges and houses —and these were only the beginning.

"I am well satisfied," he said. "We have, as we planned, diverted the whole stream of our culture, turning it away from the dangers that lay ahead. The powers that made the Madness possible will soon be forgotten: only a handful of us still know of them, and we will take our secrets with us. Perhaps when our descendants rediscover them they will be wise enough to use them properly. But we have uncovered so many new wonders that it may be a thousand generations before we turn again to look into our own minds and to tamper with the forces locked within them."

The mouth of the cave was illuminated by a sudden flash of lightning. The storm was coming nearer, though it was still some miles away. Rain was beginning to fall in large, angry drops from the leaden sky.

"While we're waiting for the ships," said Aretenon rather abruptly, "come into the next cave and see some of the new things we have to show you since your last visit."

It was a strange collection. Side by side on the same bench were tools and inventions which in other cultures had been separated by thousands of years of time. The Stone Age was past: bronze and iron had come, and already the first crude scientific instruments had been built for experiments that were driving back the frontiers of the unknown. A primitive retort spoke of the beginnings of chemistry, and by its side were the first lenses that the world had seen—waiting to reveal the unsuspected universes of the infinitely small and the infinitely great.

The storm was upon them as Aretenon's description of these new wonders drew to a close. From time to time he had glanced nervously at the mouth of the cave, as if awaiting a messenger from the harbor, but they had remained undisturbed save by the occasional crash of thunder.

"I've shown you everything of importance," he said, "but here's something that may amuse you while we're waiting. As I said, we've sent expeditions everywhere to collect and classify all the rocks they can, in the hope of finding useful minerals. One of them brought back this."

He extinguished the lights and the cave became completely dark.

"It will be some time before your eyes grow sensitive

enough to see it," Aretenon warned. "Just look over there in that corner."

Eris strained his eyes into the darkness. At first he could see nothing: then, slowly, a glimmering blue light became faintly visible. It was so vague and diffuse that he could not focus his eyes upon it, and he automatically moved forward.

"I shouldn't go too near," advised Aretenon. "It seems to be a perfectly ordinary mineral, but the Phileni who found it and carried it here got some very strange burns from handling it. Yet it's quite cold to the touch. One day we'll learn its secret: but I don't suppose it's anything at all important."

A vast curtain of sheet-lightning split the sky, and for a moment the reflected glare lighted up the cave, pinning weird shadows against the walls. At the same moment one of the Phileni staggered into the entrance and called something to Aretenon in his thin, reedy voice. He gave a great shout of triumph, as one of his ancestors might have done on some ancient battlefield: then his thoughts came crashing into Eris's mind.

"Land! They've found land—a whole new continent waiting for us!"

Eris felt the sense of triumph and victory well up within him like water bursting from a spring. Clear ahead now into the future lay the new, the glorious road along which their children would travel, mastering the world and all its secrets as they went. The vision of Therodimus was at last sharp and brilliant before his eyes.

He felt for the mind of Jeryl, so that she could share his joy—and found that it was closed to him. Leaning toward her in the darkness, he could sense that she was still staring into the depths of the cave, as if she had never heard the wonderful news, and could not tear her eyes away from the enigmatic glow.

Out of the night came the roar of the belated thunder as it raced across the sky. Eris felt Jeryl tremble beside him, and sent out his thoughts to comfort her.

"Don't let the thunder frighten you," he said gently. "What is there to fear now?"

"I do not know," replied Jeryl. "I am frightened—but not of the thunder. Oh, Eris, it is a wonderful thing we have done, and I wish that Therodimus could be here to see it. But where will it lead in the end—this new road of ours?"

Out of the past, the words that Aretenon had once spoken had risen up to haunt her. She remembered their walk by the river, long ago, when he had talked of his hopes and had asked: "Certainly nothing we can learn from Nature will ever be as great a threat as the peril we have uncovered in our own minds." Now the words seemed to mock her and to cast a shadow over the golden future: but why, she could not say.

Alone, perhaps, of all the races in the Universe, her people had reached the second crossroads—and had never passed the first. Now they must go along the road that they had missed, and must face the challenge at its end—the challenge from which, this time, they could not escape.

In the darkness, the faint glow of dying atoms burned unwavering in the rock. It would still be burning there, scarcely dimmed, when Jeryl and Eris had been dust for centuries. It would be only a little fainter when the civilization they were building had at last unlocked its secrets.

"If I Forget Thee,
Oh Earth . . . "

When Marvin was ten years old, his father took him through the long, echoing corridors that led up through Administration and Power, until at last they came to the uppermost levels of all and were among the swiftly growing vegetation of the Farmlands. Marvin liked it here: it was fun watching the great, slender plants creeping with almost visible eagerness toward the sunlight as it filtered down through the plastic domes to meet them. The smell of life was everywhere, awakening inexpressible longings in his heart: no longer was he breathing the dry, cool air of the residential levels, purged of all smells but the faint tang of ozone. He wished he could stay here for a little while, but Father would not let him. They went onward until they had reached the entrance to the Observatory, which he had never visited: but they did not stop, and Marvin knew with a sense of rising excitement that there could be only one goal left. For the first time in his life, he was going Outside.

There were a dozen of the surface vehicles, with their wide balloon tires and pressurized cabins, in the great servicing chamber. His father must have been expected, for they were led at once to the little scout car waiting by the huge circular door of the airlock. Tense with expectancy, Marvin settled himself down in the cramped cabin while his father started the motor and checked the controls. The inner door of the lock slid open and then closed behind them: he heard the roar of the great air pumps fade slowly away as the pressure dropped to zero.

Then the "Vacuum" sign flashed on, the outer door parted, and before Marvin lay the land which he had never yet entered.

He had seen it in photographs, of course: he had watched it imaged on television screens a hundred times. But now it was lying all around him, burning beneath the fierce sun that crawled so slowly across the jet-black sky. He stared into the west, away from the blinding splendor of the sun—and there were the stars, as he had been told but had never quite believed. He gazed at them for a long time, marveling that anything could be so bright and yet so tiny. They were intense unscintillating points, and suddenly he remembered a rhyme he had once read in one of his father's books:

> Twinkle, twinkle, little star,
> How I wonder what you are.

Well, he knew what the stars were. Whoever asked that question must have been very stupid. And what did they mean by "twinkle"? You could see at a glance that all the stars shone with the same steady, unwavering light. He abandoned the puzzle and turned his attention to the landscape around him.

They were racing across a level plain at almost a hundred miles an hour, the great balloon tires sending up little spurts of dust behind them. There was no sign of the Colony: in the few minutes while he had been gazing at the stars, its domes and radio towers had fallen below the horizon. Yet there were other indications of man's presence, for about a mile ahead Marvin could see the curiously shaped structures clustering round the head of a mine. Now and then a puff of vapor would emerge from a squat smokestack and would instantly disperse.

They were past the mine in a moment: Father was driving with a reckless and exhilarating skill as if—it was a strange thought to come into a child's mind—he were trying to escape from something. In a few minutes they had reached the edge of the plateau on which the Colony had been built. The ground fell sharply away beneath them in a dizzying slope whose lower stretches were lost in shadow. Ahead, as far as the eye could reach, was a jumbled wasteland of craters, mountain ranges, and ravines. The crests of the mountains, catching the low sun, burned like islands of fire in a sea of darkness: and above them the stars still shone as steadfastly as ever.

There could be no way forward—yet there was. Marvin clenched his fists as the car edged over the slope and started the long descent. Then he saw the barely visible track leading down the mountainside, and relaxed a little. Other men, it seemed, had gone this way before.

Night fell with a shocking abruptness as they crossed the shadow line and the sun dropped below the crest of the plateau. The twin searchlights sprang into life, casting blue-white bands on the rocks ahead, so that there was scarcely need to check their speed. For hours they drove through valleys and past the foot of mountains whose peaks seemed to comb the stars, and sometimes they emerged for a moment into the sunlight as they climbed over higher ground.

And now on the right was a wrinkled, dusty plain, and on the left, its ramparts and terraces rising mile after mile into the sky, was a wall of mountains that marched into the distance until its peaks sank from sight below the rim of the world. There was no sign that men had ever explored this land, but once they passed the skeleton of a crashed rocket, and beside it a stone cairn surmounted by a metal cross.

It seemed to Marvin that the mountains stretched on forever: but at last, many hours later, the range ended in a towering, precipitous headland that rose steeply from a cluster of little hills. They drove down into a shallow valley that curved in a great arc toward the far side of the mountains: and as they did so, Marvin slowly realized that something very strange was happening in the land ahead.

The sun was now low behind the hills on the right: the valley before them should be in total darkness. Yet it was awash with a cold white radiance that came spilling over the crags beneath which they were driving.

Then, suddenly, they were out in the open plain, and the source of the light lay before them in all its glory.

It was very quiet in the little cabin now that the motors had stopped. The only sound was the faint whisper of the oxygen feed and an occasional metallic crepitation as the outer walls of the vehicle radiated away their heat. For no warmth at all came from the great silver crescent that floated low above the far horizon and flooded all this land with pearly light. It was so brilliant that minutes passed before Marvin could accept its challenge and look steadfastly into its glare, but at last he could discern the outlines of continents, the hazy border of the atmosphere, and the white islands of cloud. And even at this distance, he could see the glitter of sunlight on the polar ice.

It was beautiful, and it called to his heart across the abyss of space. There in that shining crescent were all the wonders that he had never known—the hues of sunset skies, the moaning of the sea on pebbled shores, the patter of falling rain, the unhurried benison of snow. These and a thousand others should have been his rightful heritage, but he knew them only from the books and ancient records, and the thought filled him with the anguish of exile.

Why could they not return? It seemed so peaceful beneath those lines of marching cloud. Then Marvin, his eyes no longer blinded by the glare, saw that the portion of the disk that should have been in darkness was gleaming faintly with an evil phosphorescence: and he remembered. He was looking upon the funeral pyre of a world—upon the radioactive aftermath of Armageddon. Across a quarter of a million miles of space, the glow of dying atoms was still visible, a perennial reminder of the ruinous past. It would be centuries yet before that deadly glow died from the rocks and life could return again to fill that silent, empty world.

And now Father began to speak, telling Marvin the story which until this moment had meant no more to him than the fairy tales he had once been told. There were many things he could not understand: it was impossible for him to picture the glowing, multicolored pattern of life on the planet he had never seen. Nor could he comprehend the forces that had destroyed it in the end, leaving the Colony, preserved by its isolation, as the sole survivor. Yet he could share the agony of those final days, when the Colony had learned at last that never again would the supply ships come flaming down through the stars with gifts from home. One by one the radio stations had ceased to call: on the shadowed globe the lights of the cities had dimmed and died, and they were alone at last, as no men had ever been alone before, carrying in their hands the future of the race.

Then had followed the years of despair, and the long-drawn battle for survival in this fierce and hostile world. That battle had been won, though barely: this little oasis of life was safe against the worst that Nature could do. But unless there was a goal, a future toward which it could work, the Colony would lose the will to live, and neither machines nor skill nor science could save it then.

So, at last, Marvin understood the purpose of this pilgrimage. He would never walk beside the rivers of that lost and legendary world, or listen to the thunder raging above its softly rounded hills. Yet one day—how far ahead?—his children's children would return to claim their heritage. The winds and the rains would scour the poisons from the burning lands and carry them to the sea, and in the depths of the sea they would waste their venom until they could harm no living things. Then the great ships that were still waiting here on the silent, dusty plains could lift once more into space, along the road that led to home.

That was the dream: and one day, Marvin knew with a sudden flash of insight, he would pass it on to his own son, here at this same spot with the mountains behind him and the silver light from the sky streaming into his face.

He did not look back as they began the homeward journey. He could not bear to see the cold glory of the crescent Earth fade from the rocks around him, as he went to rejoin his people in their long exile.

Breaking Strain

Grant was writing up the *Star Queen's* log when he heard the cabin door opening behind him. He didn't bother to look round—it was hardly necessary for there was only one other man aboard the ship. But when nothing happened, and when McNeil neither spoke nor came into the room, the long silence finally roused Grant's curiosity and he swung the seat round in its gimbals.

McNeil was just standing in the doorway, looking as if he had seen a ghost. The trite metaphor flashed into Grant's mind instantly. He did not know for a moment how near the truth it was. In a sense McNeil *had* seen a ghost—the most terrifying of all ghosts—his own.

"What's the matter?" said Grant angrily. "You sick or something?"

The engineer shook his head. Grant noticed the little beads of sweat that broke away from his forehead and went glittering across the room on their perfectly straight trajectories. His throat muscles moved, but for a while no sound came. It looked as though he was going to cry.

"We're done for," he whispered at last. "Oxygen reserve's gone."

Then he did cry. He looked like a flabby doll, slowly

41

collapsing on itself. He couldn't fall, for there was no
gravity, so he just folded up in mid-air.

Grant said nothing. Quite unconsciously he rammed
his smoldering cigarette into the ash tray, grinding it
viciously until the last tiny spark had died. Already the
air seemed to be thickening around him as the oldest
terror of the spaceways gripped him by the throat.

He slowly loosed the elastic straps which, while he
was seated, gave some illusion of weight, and with an
automatic skill launched himself toward the doorway.
McNeil did not offer to follow. Even making every al-
lowance for the shock he had undergone, Grant felt that
he was behaving very badly. He gave the engineer an
angry cuff as he passed and told him to snap out of it.

The hold was a large hemispherical room with a thick
central column which carried the controls and cabling to
the other half of the dumb-bell-shaped spaceship a hundred meters away. It was packed with crates and boxes
arranged in a surrealistic three-dimensional array that
made very few concessions to gravity.

But even if the cargo had suddenly vanished Grant
would scarcely have noticed. He had eyes only for the
big oxygen tank, taller than himself, which was bolted
against the wall near the inner door of the airlock.

It was just as he had last seen it, gleaming with alumi-
num paint, and the metal sides still held the faint touch
of coldness that gave the only hint of the contents. All
the piping seemed in perfect condition. There was no
sign of anything wrong apart from one minor detail. The
needle of the contents gauge lay mutely against the zero
stop.

Grant gazed at that silent symbol as a man in ancient
London, returning home one evening at the time of the
Plague, might have stared at a rough cross newly
scrawled upon his door. Then he banged half a dozen
times on the glass in the futile hope that the needle had
stuck—though he never really doubted its message.
News that is sufficiently bad somehow carries its own
guarantee of truth. Only good reports need confirmation.

When Grant got back to the control room, McNeil was himself again. A glance at the opened medicine chest showed the reason for the engineer's rapid recovery. He even assayed a faint attempt at humor.

"It was a meteor," he said. "They tell us a ship this size should get hit once a century. We seem to have jumped the gun with ninety-five years still to go."

"But what about the alarms? The air pressure's normal —how could we have been holed?"

"We weren't," McNeil replied. "You know how the oxygen circulates night-side through the refrigerating coils to keep it liquid? The meteor must have smashed them and the stuff simply boiled away."

Grant was silent, collecting his thoughts. What had happened was serious—deadly serious—but it need not be fatal. After all, the voyage was more than three quarters over.

"Surely the regenerator can keep the air breathable, even if it does get pretty thick?" he asked hopefully.

McNeil shook his head. "I've not worked it out in detail, but I know the answer. When the carbon dioxide is broken down and the free oxygen gets cycled back there's a loss of about ten per cent. That's why we have to carry a reserve."

"The space suits!" cried Grant in sudden excitement. "What about their tanks?"

He had spoken without thinking, and the immediate realization of his mistake left him feeling worse than before.

"We can't keep oxygen in them—it would boil off in a few days. There's enough compressed gas there for about thirty minutes—merely long enough for you to get to the main tank in an emergency."

"There must be a way out—even if we have to jettison cargo and run for it. Let's stop guessing and work out exactly where we are."

Grant was as much angry as frightened. He was angry with McNeil for breaking down. He was angry with the designers of the ship for not having foreseen this God-knew-how-many-million-to-one-chance. The deadline might be a couple of weeks away and a lot could happen before then. The thought helped for a moment to keep his fears at arm's length.

This was an emergency, beyond doubt, but it was one of those peculiarly protracted emergencies that seem to happen only in space. There was plenty of time to think —perhaps too much time.

Grant strapped himself in the pilot's seat and pulled out a writing-pad.

"Let's get the facts right," he said with artificial calmness. "We've got the air that's still circulating in the ship and we lose ten per cent of the oxygen every time it goes through the generator. Chuck me over the Manual, will you? I can never remember how many cubic meters we use a day."

In saying that the *Star Queen* might expect to be hit by a meteor once every century, McNeil had grossly but unavoidably oversimplified the problem. For the answer depended on so many factors that three generations of statisticians had done little but lay down rules so vague that the insurance companies still shivered with apprehension when the great meteor showers went sweeping like a gale through the orbits of the inner worlds.

Everything depends, of course, on what one means by the word meteor. Each lump of cosmic slag that reaches the surface of the Earth has a million smaller brethren that perish utterly in the no-man's-land where the atmosphere has not quite ended and space has yet to begin—that ghostly region where the weird Aurora sometimes walks by night.

These are the familiar shooting stars, seldom larger than a pin's head, and these in turn are outnumbered a millionfold again by particles too small to leave any visible trace of their dying as they drift down from the sky. All of them, the countless specks of dust, the rare boulders and even the wandering mountains that Earth encounters perhaps once every million years—all of them are meteors.

For the purposes of space-flight, a meteor is only of interest if, on penetrating the hull of a ship, it leaves a hole large enough to be dangerous. This is a matter of relative speeds as well as size. Tables have been prepared showing approximate collision times for various parts of the Solar System—and for various sizes of meteors down to masses of a few milligrams.

That which had struck the *Star Queen* was a giant, being nearly a centimeter across and weighing all of ten grams. According to the table the waiting-time for collision with such a monster was of the order of ten to the ninth days—say three million years. The virtual certainty that such an occurrence would not happen again in the course of human history gave Grant and McNeil very little consolation.

However, things might have been worse. The *Star Queen* was 115 days on her orbit and had only 30 still to go. She was traveling, as did all freighters, on the long tangential ellipse kissing the orbits of Earth and Venus on opposite sides of the Sun. The fast liners could cut across from planet to planet at three times her speed—and ten times her fuel consumption—but she must plod along her predetermined track like a streetcar, taking 145 days, more or less, for each journey.

Anything more unlike the early-twentieth-century idea of a spaceship than the *Star Queen* would be hard to imagine. She consisted of two spheres, one fifty and the other twenty meters in diameter, joined by a cylinder about a hundred meters long. The whole structure looked like a match-stick-and-Plasticine model of a hydrogen atom. Crew, cargo, and controls were in the larger sphere, while the smaller one held the atomic motors and was—to put it mildly—out of bounds to living matter.

The *Star Queen* had been built in space and could never have lifted herself even from the surface of the Moon. Under full power her ion drive could produce an acceleration of a twentieth of a gravity, which in an hour would give her all the velocity she needed to change from a satellite of the Earth to one of Venus.

Hauling cargo up from the planets was the job of the powerful little chemical rockets. In a month the tugs would be climbing up from Venus to meet her, but the *Star Queen* would not be stopping for there would be no one at the controls. She would continue blindly on her orbit, speeding past Venus at miles a second—and five months later she would be back at the orbit of the Earth, though Earth itself would then be far away.

It is surprising how long it takes to do a simple addition when your life depends on the answer. Grant ran down the short column of figures half a dozen times before he finally gave up hope that the total would change. Then he sat doodling nervously on the white plastic of the pilot's desk.

"With all possible economies," he said, "we can last about twenty days. That means we'll be ten days out of Venus when. . . ." His voice trailed off into silence.

Ten days didn't sound much—but it might just as well have been ten years. Grant thought sardonically of all the hack adventure writers who had used just this situation in their stories and radio serials. In these circumstances, according to the carbon-copy experts—few of whom had ever gone beyond the Moon—there were three things that could happen.

The popular solution—which had become almost a cliché—was to turn the ship into a glorified greenhouse or a hydroponic farm and let photosynthesis do the rest. Alternatively one could perform prodigies of chemical or atomic engineering—explained in tedious technical detail—and build an oxygen manufacturing plant which would not only save your life—and of course the heroine's —but also make you the owner of fabulously valuable patents. The third or *deus ex machina* solution was the arrival of a convenient spaceship which happened to be matching your course and velocity exactly.

But that was fiction and things were different in real life. Although the first idea was sound in theory there wasn't even a packet of grass seed aboard the *Star Queen*. As for feats of inventive engineering, two men—however brilliant and however desperate—were not likely to improve in a few days on the work of scores of great industrial research organizations over a full century.

The spaceship that "happened to be passing" was, almost by definition, impossible. Even if other freighters had been coasting on the same elliptic path—and Grant knew there were none—then by the very laws that governed their movements they would always keep their original separations. It was not quite impossible that a liner, racing on its hyperbolic orbit, might pass within a few hundred thousand kilometers of them—but at a speed so great that it would be as inaccessible as Pluto.

"If we threw out the cargo," said McNeil at last, "would we have a chance of changing our orbit?"

Grant shook his head.

"I'd hoped so," he replied, "but it won't work. We could reach Venus in a week if we wished—but we'd have no fuel for braking and nothing from the planet could catch us as we went past."

"Not even a liner?"

"According to *Lloyd's Register* Venus has only a couple of freighters at the moment. In any case it would be a practically impossible maneuver. Even if it could match our speed how would the rescue ship get back? It would need about fifty kilometers a second for the whole job!"

"If we can't figure a way out," said McNeil, "maybe someone on Venus can. We'd better talk to them."

"I'm going to," Grant replied, "as soon as I've decided what to say. Go and get the transmitter aligned, will you?"

He watched McNeil as he floated out of the room. The engineer was probably going to give trouble in the days that lay ahead. Until now they had got on well enough—like most stout men McNeil was good-natured and easygoing. But now Grant realized that he lacked fiber. He had become flabby—physically and mentally—living too long in space.

A buzzer sounded on the transmitter switchboard. The

parabolic mirror out on the hull was aimed at the gleaming arc-lamp of Venus, only ten million kilometers away and moving on an almost parallel path. The three-millimeter waves from the ship's transmitter would make the trip in little more than half a minute. There was bitterness in the knowledge that they were only thirty seconds from safety.

The automatic monitor on Venus gave its impersonal *Go ahead* signal and Grant began to talk steadily, and he hoped, quite dispassionately. He gave a careful analysis of the situation and ended with a request for advice. His fears concerning McNeil he left unspoken. For one thing he knew that the engineer would be monitoring him at the transmitter.

As yet no one on Venus would have heard the message, even though the transmission time-lag was over. It would still be coiled up in the recorder spools, but in a few minutes an unsuspecting signal officer would arrive to play it over.

He would have no idea of the bombshell that was about to burst, triggering trains of sympathetic ripples on all the inhabited worlds as television and newssheet took up the refrain. An accident in space has a dramatic quality that crowds all other items from the headlines.

Until now Grant had been too preoccupied with his own safety to give much thought to the cargo in his charge. A sea captain of ancient times, whose first thought was for his ship, might have been shocked by this attitude. Grant, however, had reason on his side.

The *Star Queen* could never founder, could never run upon uncharted rocks or pass silently, as so many ships have passed, forever from the knowledge of man. She was safe, whatever might befall her crew. If she was undisturbed she would continue to retrace her orbit with such precision that men might set their calendars by her for centuries to come.

The cargo, Grant suddenly remembered, was insured for over twenty million dollars. There were not many goods valuable enough to be shipped from world to world and most of the crates in the hold were worth more than their weight—or rather their mass—in gold. Perhaps some items might be useful in this emergency and Grant went to the safe to find the loading schedule.

He was sorting the thin, tough sheets when McNeil came back into the cabin.

"I've been reducing the air pressure," he said. "The hull shows some leaks that wouldn't have mattered in the usual way."

Grant nodded absently as he passed a bundle of sheets over to McNeil.

"Here's our loading schedule. I suggest we both run through it in case there's anything in the cargo that may help."

If it did nothing else, he might have added, it would at least give them something to occupy their minds.

As he ran down the long columns of numbered items —a complete cross-section of interplanetary commerce— Grant found himself wondering what lay behind these inanimate symbols. *Item 347 - 1 book - 4 kilos gross.*

He whistled as he noticed that it was a starred item, insured for a hundred thousand dollars, and he suddenly remembered hearing on the radio that the Hesperian Museum had just bought a first edition *Seven Pillars of Wisdom.*

A few sheets later was a very contrasting item, *Miscellaneous books—25 kilos—no intrinsic value.*

It had cost a small fortune to ship those books to Venus, yet they were of "no intrinsic value." Grant let his imagination loose on the problem. Perhaps someone who was leaving Earth forever was taking with him to a new world his most cherished treasures—the dozen or so volumes that above all others had most shaped his mind.

Item 564 - 12 reels film.

That, of course, would be the Neronian super-epic, *While Rome Burns,* which had left Earth just one jump ahead of the censor. Venus was waiting for it with considerable impatience.

Medical supplies - 50 kilos. Case of cigars - 1 kilo. Precision instruments - 75 kilos. So the list went on. Each item was something rare or something which the industry and science of a younger civilization could not yet produce.

The cargo was sharply divided into two classes—blatant luxury or sheer necessity. There was little in between. And there was nothing, nothing at all, which gave Grant the slightest hope. He did not see how it could have been otherwise, but that did not prevent him from feeling a quite unreasonable disappointment.

The reply from Venus, when it came at last, took nearly an hour to run through the recorder. It was a questionnaire so detailed that Grant wondered morosely if he'd live long enough to answer it. Most of the queries were technical ones concerning the ship. The experts on two planets were pooling their brains in the attempt to save the *Star Queen* and her cargo.

"Well, what do you think of it?" Grant asked McNeil when the other had finished running through the message. He was watching the engineer carefully for any further sign of strain.

There was a long pause before McNeil spoke. Then he shrugged his shoulders and his first words were an echo of Grant's own thoughts.

"It will certainly keep us busy. I won't be able to do all these tests in under a day. I can see what they're driving at most of the time, but some of the questions are just plain crazy."

Grant had suspected that, but said nothing as the other continued.

"Rate of hull leakage—that's sensible enough, but why should anyone want to know the efficiency of our radiation screening? I think they're trying to keep up our morale by pretending they have some bright ideas—or else they want to keep us too busy to worry."

Grant was relieved and yet annoyed by McNeil's calmness—relieved because he had been afraid of another scene and annoyed because McNeil was not fitting at all neatly into the mental category he had prepared for him. Was that first momentary lapse typical of the man or might it have happened to anyone?

Grant, to whom the world was very much a place of

blacks and whites, felt angry at being unable to decide whether McNeil was cowardly or courageous. That he might be both was a possibility that never occurred to him.

There is a timelessness about space-flight that is unmatched by any other experience of man. Even on the Moon there are shadows that creep sluggishly from crag to crag as the sun makes its slow march across the sky. Earthward there is always the great clock of the spinning globe, marking the hours with continents for hands. But on a long voyage in a gyro-stabilized ship the same patterns of sunlight lie unmoving on wall or floor as the chronometer ticks off its meaningless hours and days.

Grant and McNeil had long since learned to regulate their lives accordingly. In deep space they moved and thought with a leisureliness that would vanish quickly enough when a voyage was nearing its end and the time for braking maneuvers had arrived. Though they were now under sentence of death, they continued along the well-worn grooves of habit.

Every day Grant carefully wrote up the log, checked the ship's position and carried out his various routine duties. McNeil was also behaving normally as far as could be told, though Grant suspected that some of the technical maintenance was being carried out with a very light hand.

It was now three days since the meteor had struck. For the last twenty-four hours Earth and Venus had been in conference and Grant wondered when he would hear the result of their deliberations. He did not believe that the finest technical brains in the Solar System could save them now, but it was hard to abandon hope when everything still seemed so normal and the air was still clean and fresh.

On the fourth day Venus spoke again. Shorn of its technicalities, the message was nothing more or less than a funeral oration. Grant and McNeil had been written off, but they were given elaborate instructions concerning the safety of the cargo.

Back on earth the astronomers were computing all the possible rescue orbits that might make contact with the *Star Queen* in the next few years. There was even a chance that she might be reached from Earth six or seven months later, when she was back at aphelion, but the maneuver could be carried out only by a fast liner with no payload and would cost a fortune in fuel.

McNeil vanished soon after this message came through. At first Grant was a little relieved. If McNeil chose to look after himself that was his own affair. Besides there were various letters to write—though the last-will-and-testament business could come later.

It was McNeil's turn to prepare the "evening" meal, a duty he enjoyed for he took good care of his stomach. When the usual sounds from the galley were not forthcoming Grant went in search of his crew.

He found McNeil lying in his bunk, very much at peace with the universe. Hanging in the air beside him was a large metal crate which had been roughly forced open. Grant had no need to examine it closely to guess its contents. A glance at McNeil was enough.

"It's a dirty shame," said the engineer without a trace of embarrassment, "to suck this stuff up through a tube. Can't you put on some 'g' so that we can drink it properly?"

Grant stared at him with angry contempt, but McNeil returned his gaze unabashed.

Oh, don't be a sourpuss! Have some yourself—what does it matter now?

He pushed across a bottle and Grant fielded it deftly as it floated by. It was a fabulously valuable wine—he remembered the consignment now—and the contents of that small crate must be worth thousands.

"I don't think there's any need," said Grant severely, "to behave like a pig—even in these circumstances."

McNeil wasn't drunk yet. He had only reached the brightly lighted anteroom of intoxication and had not lost all contact with the drab outer world.

"I am prepared," he said with great solemnity, "to

listen to any good argument against my present course of action—a course which seems eminently sensible to me. But you'd better convince me quickly while I'm still amenable to reason."

He pressed the plastic bulb again and a purple jet shot into his mouth.

"Apart from the fact that you're stealing Company property which will certainly be salvaged sooner or later —you can hardly stay drunk for several weeks."

"That," said McNeil thoughtfully, "remains to be seen."

"I don't think so," retorted Grant. Bracing himself against the wall, he gave the crate a vicious shove that sent it flying through the open doorway.

As he dived after it and slammed the door he heard McNeil shout, "Well, of all the dirty tricks!"

It would take the engineer some time—particularly in his present condition—to unbuckle himself and follow. Grant steered the crate back to the hold and locked the door. As there was never any need to lock the hold when the ship was in space McNeil wouldn't have a key for it himself and Grant could hide the duplicate that was kept in the control cabin.

McNeil was singing when, some time later, Grant went back past his room. He still had a couple of bottles for company and was shouting:

> "We don't care *where* the oxygen goes
> If it doesn't get into the wine. . . ."

Grant, whose education had been severely technical, couldn't place the quotation. As he paused to listen he suddenly found himself shaken by an emotion which, to do him justice, he did not for a moment recognize.

It passed as swiftly as it had come, leaving him sick and trembling. For the first time, he realized that his dislike of McNeil was slowly turning to hatred.

It is a fundamental rule of space-flight that, for sound psychological reasons, the minimum crew on a long journey shall consist of not less than three men.

But rules are made to be broken and the *Star Queen's* owners had obtained full authority from the Board of Space Control and the insurance companies when the freighter set off for Venus without her regular captain.

At the last moment he had been taken ill and there was no replacement. Since the planets are disinclined to wait upon man and his affairs, if she did not sail on time she would not sail at all.

Millions of dollars were involved—so she sailed. Grant and McNeil were both highly capable men and they had no objection at all to earning double their normal pay for very little extra work. Despite fundamental differences in temperament, they got on well enough in ordinary circumstances. It was nobody's fault that circumstances were now very far from ordinary.

Three days without food, it is said, is long enough to remove most of the subtle differences between a civilized man and a savage. Grant and McNeil were still in no physical discomfort. But their imaginations had been only too active and they now had more in common with two hungry Pacific Islanders in a lost canoe than either would have cared to admit.

For there was one aspect of the situation, and that the most important of all, which had never been mentioned. When the last figures on Grant's writing-pad had been checked and rechecked, the calculation was still not quite complete. Instantly each man had made the one further step, each had arrived simultaneously at the same unspoken result.

It was terribly simple—a macabre parody of those problems in first-year arithmetic that begin, "If six men take two days to assemble five helicopters, how long . . ."

The oxygen would last *two* men for about twenty days, and Venus was thirty days away. One did not have to be a calculating prodigy to see at once that one man, and one man only, might yet live to walk the metal streets of Port Hesperus.

The acknowledged deadline was twenty days ahead, but the unmentioned one was only ten days off. Until that time there would still be enough air for two men—

and thereafter for one man only for the rest of the voyage.
To a sufficiently detached observer the situation would
have been very entertaining.

It was obvious that the conspiracy of silence could not
last much longer. But it is not easy, even at the best of
times, for two people to decide amicably which one of
them shall commit suicide. It is still more difficult when
they are no longer on speaking terms.

Grant wished to be perfectly fair. Therefore the only
thing to do was to wait until McNeil sobered up and then
to put the question to him frankly. He could think best
at his desk, so he went to the control cabin and strapped
himself down in the pilot's chair.

For a while he stared thoughtfully into nothingness. It
would be better, he decided, to broach the matter by
correspondence, especially while diplomatic relations
were in their present state. He clipped a sheet of note-
paper on the writing-pad and began, "Dear McNeil . . ."
Then he tore it out and started again, "McNeil . . ."

It took him the best part of three hours and even then
he wasn't wholly satisfied. There were some things it was
so darned difficult to put down on paper. But at last he
managed to finish. He sealed the letter and locked it away
in his safe. It could wait for a day or two.

Few of the waiting millions on Earth and Venus could
have any idea of the tensions that were slowly building
up aboard the *Star Queen.* For days press and radio had
been full of fantastic rescue schemes. On three worlds
there was hardly any other topic of conversation. But
only the faintest echo of the planet-wide tumult reached
the two men who were its cause.

At any time the station on Venus could speak to the
Star Queen, but there was so little that could be said.
One could not with any decency give words of encour-
agement to men in the condemned cell, even when there
was some slight uncertainty about the actual date of
execution.

So Venus contented itself with a few routine messages
every day and blocked the steady stream of exhortations

and newspaper offers that came pouring in from Earth. As a result private radio companies on Earth made frantic attempts to contact the *Star Queen* directly. They failed, simply because it never occurred to Grant and McNeil to focus their receiver anywhere except on Venus, now so tantalizingly near at hand.

There had been an embarrassing interlude when McNeil emerged from his cabin, but though relations were not particularly cordial, life aboard the *Star Queen* continued much as before.

Grant spent most of his waking hours in the pilot's position, calculating approach maneuvers and writing interminable letters to his wife. He could have spoken to her had he wished, but the thought of all those millions of waiting ears had prevented him from doing so. Interplanetary speech circuits were supposed to be private—but too many people would be interested in this one.

In a couple of days, Grant assured himself, he would hand his letter to McNeil and they could decide what was to be done. Such a delay would also give McNeil a chance of raising the subject himself. That he might have other reasons for his hesitation was something Grant's conscious mind still refused to admit.

He often wondered how McNeil was spending his time. The engineer had a large library of microfilm books, for he read widely and his range of interests was unusual. His favorite book, Grant knew, was *Jurgen* and perhaps even now he was trying to forget his doom by losing himself in its strange magic. Others of McNeil's books were less respectable and not a few were of the class curiously described as "curious."

The truth of the matter was that McNeil was far too subtle and complicated a personality for Grant to understand. He was a hedonist and enjoyed the pleasures of life all the more for being cut off from them for months at a time. But he was by no means the moral weakling that the unimaginative and somewhat puritanical Grant had supposed.

It was true that he had collapsed completely under the initial shock and that his behavior over the wine was—by Grant's standards—reprehensible. But McNeil had had his breakdown and had recovered. Therein lay the difference between him and the hard but brittle Grant.

Though the normal routine of duties had been resumed by tacit consent, it did little to reduce the sense of strain. Grant and McNeil avoided each other as much as possible except when mealtimes brought them together. When they did meet, they behaved with an exaggerated politeness as if each were striving to be perfectly normal —and inexplicably failing.

Grant had hoped that McNeil would himself broach the subject of suicide, thus sparing him a very awkward duty. When the engineer stubbornly refused to do anything of the sort it added to Grant's resentment and contempt. To make matters worse he was now suffering from nightmares and sleeping very badly.

The nightmare was always the same. When he was a child it had often happened that at bedtime he had been reading a story far too exciting to be left until morning. To avoid detection he had continued reading under the bedclothes by flashlight, curled up in a snug white-walled cocoon. Every ten minutes or so the air had become too stifling to breathe and his emergence into the delicious cool air had been a major part of the fun.

Now, thirty years later, these innocent childhood hours returned to haunt him. He was dreaming that he could not escape from the suffocating sheets while the air was steadily and remorselessly thickening around him.

He had intended to give McNeil the letter after two days, yet somehow he put it off again. This procrastination was very unlike Grant, but he managed to persuade himself that it was a perfectly reasonable thing to do.

He was giving McNeil a chance to redeem himself— to prove that he wasn't a coward by raising the matter himself. That McNeil might be waiting for him to do exactly the same thing somehow never occurred to Grant.

The all-too-literal deadline was only five days off when, for the first time, Grant's mind brushed lightly against the thought of murder. He had been sitting after the

"evening" meal, trying to relax as McNeil clattered around
in the galley with, he considered, quite unnecessary noise.

What use, he asked himself, was the engineer to the
world? He had no responsibilities and no family—no one
would be any the worse off for his death. Grant, on the
other hand, had a wife and three children of whom he
was moderately fond, though for some obscure reason
they responded with little more than dutiful affection.

Any impartial judge would have no difficulty in de-
ciding which of them should survive. If McNeil had a
spark of decency in him he would have come to the same
conclusion already. Since he appeared to have done nothing of the sort he had forfeited all further claims to con-
sideration.

Such was the elemental logic of Grant's subconscious
mind, which had arrived at its answer days before but
had only now succeeded in attracting the attention for
which it had been clamoring. To Grant's credit he at once
rejected the thought with horror.

He was an upright and honorable person with a very
strict code of behavior. Even the vagrant homicidal impulses of what is misleadingly called "normal" man had
seldom ruffled his mind. But in the days—the very few
days—left to him, they would come more and more often.

The air had now become noticeably fouler. Though
there was still no real difficulty in breathing, it was a
constant reminder of what lay ahead, and Grant found
that it was keeping him from sleep. This was not pure
loss, as it helped to break the power of his nightmares,
but he was becoming physically run down.

His nerve was also rapidly deteriorating, a state of
affairs accentuated by the fact that McNeil seemed to
be behaving with unexpected and annoying calmness.
Grant realized that he had come to the stage when it
would be dangerous to delay the showdown any longer.

McNeil was in his room as usual when Grant went up
to the control cabin to collect the letter he had locked
away in the safe—it seemed a lifetime ago. He wondered
if he need add anything more to it. Then he realized that

this was only another excuse for delay. Resolutely he made his way toward McNeil's cabin.

A single neutron begins the chain-reaction that in an instant can destroy a million lives and the toil of generations. Equally insignificant and unimportant are the trigger-events which can sometimes change a man's course of action and so alter the whole pattern of his future.

Nothing could have been more trivial than that which made Grant pause in the corridor outside McNeil's room. In the ordinary way he would not even have noticed it. It was the smell of smoke—tobacco smoke.

The thought that the sybaritic engineer had so little self-control that he was squandering the last precious liters of oxygen in such a manner filled Grant with blinding fury. He stood for a moment quite paralyzed with the intensity of his emotion.

Then slowly, he crumpled the letter in his hand. The thought which had first been an unwelcome intruder, then a casual speculation, was at last fully accepted. McNeil had had his chance and had proved, by his unbelievable selfishness, unworthy of it. Very well—he could die.

The speed with which Grant had arrived at this conclusion would not have deceived the most amateurish of psychologists. It was relief as much as hatred that drove him away from McNeil's room. He had wanted to convince himself that there would be no need to do the honorable thing, to suggest some game of chance that would give them each an equal probability of life.

This was the excuse he needed, and he had seized upon it to salve his conscience. For though he might plan and even carry out a murder, Grant was the sort of person who would have to do it according to his own particular moral code.

As it happened he was—not for the first time—badly misjudging McNeil. The engineer was a heavy smoker and tobacco was quite essential to his mental well-being even in normal circumstances. How much more essential it was now, Grant, who only smoked occasionally and without much enjoyment, could never have appreciated.

McNeil had satisfied himself by careful calculation that four cigarettes a day would make no measurable difference whatsoever to the ship's oxygen endurance, whereas they would make all the difference in the world to his own nerves and hence indirectly to Grant's.

But it was no use explaining this to Grant. So he had smoked in private and with a self-control he found agreeably, almost voluptuously, surprising. It was sheer bad luck that Grant had detected one of the day's four cigarettes.

For a man who had only at that moment talked himself into murder, Grant's actions were remarkably methodical. Without hesitation, he hurried back to the control room and opened the medicine chest with its neatly labeled compartments, designed for almost every emergency that could occur in space.

Even the ultimate emergency had been considered, for there behind its retaining elastic bands was the tiny bottle he had been seeking, the image of which had been lying hidden far down in the unknown depths of his mind through all these days. It bore a white label carrying a skull-and-crossbones, and beneath them the words: *Approx. one-half gram will cause painless and almost instantaneous death.*

The poison was painless and instantaneous— that was good. But even more important was a fact unmentioned on the label. It was also tasteless.

The contrast between the meals prepared by Grant and those organized with considerable skill and care by McNeil was striking. Anyone who was fond of food and who spent a good deal of his life in space usually learned the art of cooking in self-defense. McNeil had done this long ago.

To Grant, on the other hand, eating was one of those necessary but annoying jobs which had to be got through as quickly as possible. His cooking reflected this opinion. McNeil had ceased to grumble about it, but he would have been very interested in the trouble Grant was taking over this particular meal.

If he noticed any increasing nervousness on Grant's part as the meal progressed, he said nothing. They ate almost in silence, but that was not unusual for they had long since exhausted most of the possibilities of light conversation. When the last dishes—deep bowls with in-turned rims to prevent the contents drifting out—had been cleared away, Grant went into the galley to prepare the coffee.

He took rather a long time, for at the last moment something quite maddening and quite ridiculous happened. He suddenly recalled one of the film classics of the last century in which the fabulous Charlie Chaplin tried to poison an unwanted wife—and then accidentally changed the glasses.

No memory could have been more unwelcome, for it left him shaken with a gust of silent hysteria. Poe's *Imp of the Perverse*, that demon who delights in defying the careful canons of self-preservation, was at work and it was a good minute before Grant could regain his self-control.

He was sure that, outwardly at least, he was quite calm as he carried in the two plastic containers and their drinking-tubes. There was no danger of confusing them, for the engineer's had the letters MAC painted boldly across it.

At the thought Grant nearly relapsed into psychopathic giggles but just managed to regain control with the somber reflection that his nerves must be in even worse condition than he had imagined.

He watched, fascinated, though without appearing to do so, as McNeil toyed with his cup. The engineer seemed in no great hurry and was staring moodily into space. Then he put his lips to the drinking tube and sipped.

A moment later he spluttered slightly—and an icy hand seemed to seize Grant's heart and hold it tight. Then McNeil turned to him and said evenly, "You've made it properly for once. It's quite hot."

Slowly, Grant's heart resumed its interrupted work.

He did not trust himself to speak, but managed a non-committal nod. McNeil parked the cup carefully in the air, a few inches away from his face.

He seemed very thoughtful, as if weighing his words for some important remark. Grant cursed himself for having made the drink so hot—that was just the sort of detail that hanged murderers. If McNeil waited much longer he would probably betray himself through nervousness.

"I suppose," said McNeil in a quietly conversational sort of way, "it has occurred to you that there's still enough air to last one of us to Venus?"

Grant forced his jangling nerves under control and tore his eyes away from that hypnotic cup. His throat seemed very dry as he answered, "It—it had crossed my mind."

McNeil touched his cup, found it still too hot and continued throughtfully, "Then wouldn't it be more sensible if one of us decided to walk out of the airlock, say— or to take some of the poison in there?" He jerked his thumb toward the medicine chest, just visible from where they were sitting.

Grant nodded.

"The only trouble, of course," added the engineer, "is to decide which of us will be the unlucky one. I suppose it would have to be by picking a card or in some other quite arbitrary way."

Grant stared at McNeil with a fascination that almost outweighed his mounting nervousness. He had never believed that the engineer could discuss the subject so calmly. Grant was sure he suspected nothing. Obviously McNeil's thoughts had been running on parallel lines to his own and it was scarcely even a coincidence that he had chosen this time, of all times, to raise the matter.

McNeil was watching him intently, as if judging his reactions.

"You're right," Grant heard himself say. "We must talk it over."

"Yes," said McNeil quite impassively. "We must." Then he reached for his cup again, put the drinking tube to his lips and sucked slowly.

Grant could not wait until he had finished. To his surprise the relief he had been expecting did not come. He even felt a stab of regret, though it was not quite remorse. It was a little late to think of it now, but he suddenly remembered that he would be alone in the *Star Queen*, haunted by his thoughts, for more than three weeks before rescue came.

He did not wish to see McNeil die, and he felt rather sick. Without another glance at his victim he launched himself toward the exit.

Immovably fixed, the fierce sun and the unwinking stars looked down upon the *Star Queen*, which seemed as motionless as they. There was no way of telling that the tiny dumbbell of the ship had now almost reached her maximum speed and that millions of horsepower were chained within the smaller sphere, waiting for the moment of its release. There was no way of telling, indeed, that she carried any life at all.

An airlock on the night-side of the ship slowly opened, letting a blaze of light escape from the interior. The brilliant circle looked very strange hanging there in the darkness. Then it was abruptly eclipsed as two figures floated out of the ship.

One was much bulkier than the other, and for a rather important reason—it was wearing a space-suit. Now there are some forms of apparel that may be worn or discarded as the fancy pleases with no other ill-effects than a possible loss of social prestige. But space-suits are not among them.

Something not easy to follow was happening in the darkness. Then the smaller figure began to move, slowly at first but with rapidly mounting speed. It swept out of the shadow of the ship into the full blast of the sun, and now one could see that strapped to its back was a small gas-cylinder from which a fine mist was jetting to vanish almost instantly into space.

It was a crude but effective rocket. There was no danger that the ship's minute gravitational pull would drag the body back to it again.

Rotating slightly, the corpse dwindled against the stars and vanished from sight in less than a minute. Quite motionless, the figure in the airlock watched it go. Then the outer door swung shut, the circle of brilliance vanished and only the pale Earthlight still glinted on the shadowed wall of the ship.

Nothing else whatsoever happened for twenty-three days.

The captain of the *Hercules* turned to his mate with a sigh of relief.

"I was afraid he couldn't do it. It must have been a colossal job to break his orbit single-handed—and with the air as thick as it must be by now. How soon can we get to him?"

"It will take about an hour. He's still got quite a bit of eccentricity but we can correct that."

"Good. Signal the *Leviathan* and *Titan* that we can make contact and ask them to take off, will you? But I wouldn't drop any tips to your news commentator friends until we're safely locked."

The mate had the grace to blush. "I don't intend to," he said in a slightly hurt voice as he pecked delicately at the keys of his calculator. The answer that flashed instantly on the screen seemed to displease him.

"We'd better board and bring the *Queen* down to circular speed ourselves before we call the other tugs," he said, "otherwise we'll be wasting a lot of fuel. She's still got a velocity excess of nearly a kilometer a second."

"Good idea—tell *Leviathan* and *Titan* to stand by but not to blast until we give them the new orbit."

While the message was on its way down through the unbroken cloudbanks that covered half the sky below, the mate remarked thoughtfully, "I wonder what he's feeling like now?"

"I can tell you. He's so pleased to be alive that he doesn't give a hoot about anything else."

"Still, I'm not sure I'd like to have left my shipmate in space so that I could get home."

"It's not the sort of thing that anyone would like to do.

But you heard the broadcast—they'd talked it over calmly and the loser went out of the airlock. It was the only sensible way."

"Sensible, perhaps—but it's pretty horrible to let someone else sacrifice himself in such a cold-blooded way so that you can live."

"Don't be a ruddy sentimentalist. I'll bet that if it happened to us you'd push me out before I could even say my prayers."

"Unless you did it to me first. Still, I don't think it's ever likely to happen to the *Hercules*. Five days out of port's the longest we've ever been, isn't it? Talk about the romance of the spaceways!"

The captain didn't reply. He was peering into the eyepiece of the navigating telescope, for the *Star Queen* should now be within optical range. There was a long pause while he adjusted the vernier controls. Then he gave a little sigh of satisfaction.

"There she is—about nine-fifty kilometers away. Tell the crew to stand by—and send a message to cheer him up. Say we'll be there in thirty minutes even if it isn't quite true."

Slowly the thousand-meter nylon ropes yielded beneath the strain as they absorbed the relative momentum of the ships, then slackened again as the *Star Queen* and the *Hercules* rebounded toward each other. The electric winches began to turn and, like a spider crawling up its thread, the *Hercules* drew alongside the freighter.

Men in space-suits sweated with heavy reaction units —tricky work, this—until the airlocks had registered and could be coupled together. The outer doors slid aside and the air in the locks mingled, fresh with foul. As the mate of the *Hercules* waited, oxygen cylinder in hand, he wondered what condition the survivor would be in. Then the *Star Queen's* inner door slid open.

For a moment, the two men stood looking at each other across the short corridor that now connected the two airlocks. The mate was surprised and a little disappointed to find that he felt no particular sense of drama.

So much had happened to make this moment possible that its actual achievement was almost an anticlimax, even in the instant when it was slipping into the past. He wished—for he was an incurable romantic—that he could think of something memorable to say, some "Doctor Livingstone, I presume?" phrase that would pass into history.

But all he actually said was, "Well, McNeil, I'm pleased to see you."

Though he was considerably thinner and somewhat haggard, McNeil had stood the ordeal well. He breathed gratefully the blast of raw oxygen and rejected the idea that he might like to lie down and sleep. As he explained, he had done very little but sleep for the last week to conserve air. The first mate looked relieved. He had been afraid he might have to wait for the story.

The cargo was being trans-shipped and the other two tugs were climbing up from the great blinding crescent of Venus while McNeil retraced the events of the last few weeks and the mate made surreptitious notes.

He spoke quite calmly and impersonally, as if he were relating some adventure that had happened to another person, or indeed had never happened at all. Which was, of course, to some extent the case, though it would be unfair to suggest that McNeil was telling any lies.

He invented nothing, but he omitted a good deal. He had had three weeks in which to prepare his narrative and he did not think it had any flaws. . . .

Grant had already reached the door when McNeil called softly after him, "What's the hurry? I thought we had something to discuss."

Grant grabbed at the doorway to halt his headlong flight. He turned slowly and stared unbelievingly at the engineer. McNeil should be already dead—but he was sitting quite comfortably, looking at him with a most peculiar expression.

"Sit down," he said sharply—and in that moment it suddenly seemed that all authority had passed to him.

Grant did so, quite without volition. Something had gone wrong, though what it was he could not imagine.

The silence in the control room seemed to last for ages. Then McNeil said rather sadly, "I'd hoped better of you, Grant."

At last Grant found his voice, though he could barely recognize it.

"What do you mean?" he whispered.

"What do you think I mean?" replied McNeil, with what seemed no more than mild irritation. "This little attempt of yours to poison me, of course."

Grant's tottering world collapsed at last, but he no longer cared greatly one way or the other. McNeil began to examine his beautifully kept fingernails with some attention.

"As a matter of interest," he said, in the way that one might ask the time, "when did you decide to kill me?"

The sense of unreality was so overwhelming that Grant felt he was acting a part, that this had nothing to do with real life at all.

"Only this morning," he said, and believed it.

"Hmm," remarked McNeil, obviously without much conviction. He rose to his feet and moved over to the medicine chest. Grant's eyes followed him as he fumbled in the compartment and came back with the little poison bottle. It still appeared to be full. Grant had been careful about that.

"I suppose I should get pretty mad about this whole business," McNeil continued conversationally, holding the bottle between thumb and forefinger. "But somehow I'm not. Maybe it's because I never had many illusions about human nature. And, of course, I saw it coming a long time ago."

Only the last phrase really reached Grant's consciousness.

"You—saw it coming?"

"Heavens, yes! You're too transparent to make a good criminal, I'm afraid. And now that your little plot's failed it leaves us both in an embarrassing position, doesn't it?"

To this masterly understatement there seemed no possible reply.

"By rights," continued the engineer thoughtfully, "I should now work myself into a good temper, call Venus Central, and denounce you to the authorities. But it would be a rather pointless thing to do, and I've never been much good at losing my temper anyway. Of course, you'll say that's because I'm too lazy—but I don't think so."

He gave Grant a twisted smile.

"Oh, I know what you think about me—you've got me neatly classified in that orderly mind of yours, haven't you? I'm soft and self-indulgent, I haven't any moral courage—or any morals for that matter—and I don't give a damn for anyone but myself. Well, I'm not denying it. Maybe it's ninety per cent true. But the odd ten per cent is mighty important, Grant!"

Grant felt in no condition to indulge in psychological analysis, and this seemed hardly the time for anything of the sort. Besides, he was still obsessed with the problem of his failure and the mystery of McNeil's continued existence. McNeil, who knew this perfectly well, seemed in no hurry to satisfy his curiosity.

"Well, what do you intend to do now?" Grant asked, anxious to get it over.

"I would like," said McNeil calmly, "to carry on our discussion where it was interrupted by the coffee."

"You don't mean—"

"But I do. Just as if nothing had happened."

"That doesn't make sense. You've got something up your sleeve!" cried Grant.

McNeil sighed. He put down the poison bottle and looked firmly at Grant.

"*You're* in no position to accuse me of plotting anything. To repeat my earlier remarks, I am suggesting that we decide which one of us shall take poison—only we don't want any more unilateral decisions. Also"—he picked up the bottle again—"it will be the real thing this time. The stuff in here merely leaves a bad taste in the mouth."

A light was beginning to dawn in Grant's mind. "You changed the poison!"

"Naturally. You may think you're a good actor, Grant, but frankly—from the balcony—I thought the performance stank. I could tell you were plotting something, probably before you knew it yourself. In the last few days I've deloused the ship pretty thoroughly. Thinking of all the ways you might have done me in was quite amusing and helped to pass the time. The poison was so obvious that it was the first thing I fixed. But I rather overdid the danger signals and nearly gave myself away when I took the first sip. Salt doesn't go at all well with coffee."

He gave that wry grin again. "Also, I'd hoped for something more subtle. So far I've found fifteen infallible ways of murdering anyone aboard a spaceship. But I don't propose to describe them now."

This was fantastic, Grant thought. He was being treated, not like a criminal, but like a rather stupid schoolboy who hadn't done his homework properly.

"Yet you're still willing," said Grant unbelievingly, "to start all over again? And you'd take the poison yourself if you lost?"

McNeil was silent for a long time. Then he began, slowly, "I can see that you still don't believe me. It doesn't fit at all nicely into your tidy little picture, does it? But perhaps I can make you understand. It's really quite simple.

"I've enjoyed life, Grant, without many scruples or regrets—but the better part of it's over now and I don't cling to what's left as desperately as you might imagine. Yet while I *am* alive I'm rather particular about some things.

"It may surprise you to know that I've got any ideals at all. But I have, Grant—I've always tried to act like a civilized, rational being. I've not always succeeded. When I've failed I've tried to redeem myself."

He paused, and when he resumed it was as though he, and not Grant, was on the defensive. "I've never exactly liked you Grant, but I've often admired you and that's why I'm sorry it's come to this. I admired you most of all the day the ship was holed."

For the first time, McNeil seemed to have some difficulty in choosing his words. When he spoke again he avoided Grant's eyes.

"I didn't behave very well then. Something happened that I thought was impossible. I've always been quite sure that I'd never lose my nerve but—well—it was so sudden it knocked me over."

He attempted to hide his embarrassment by humor. "The same sort of thing happened on my very first trip. I was sure *I'd* never be spacesick—and as a result I was much worse than if I had not been over-confident. But I got over it then—and again this time. It was one of the biggest surprises of my life, Grant, when I saw that you of all people were beginning to crack.

"Oh, yes—the business of the wines! I can see you're thinking about that. Well, that's one thing I *don't* regret. I said I'd always tried to act like a civilized man—and a civilized man should always know when to get drunk. But perhaps you wouldn't understand."

Oddly enough, that was just what Grant was beginning to do. He had caught his first real glimpse of McNeil's intricate and tortuous personality and realized how utterly he had misjudged him. No—misjudged was not the right word. In many ways his judgment had been correct. But it had only touched the surface—he had never suspected the depths that lay beneath.

In a moment of insight that had never come before, and from the nature of things could never come again, Grant understood the reasons behind McNeil's action. This was nothing so simple as a coward trying to reinstate himself in the eyes of the world, for no one need ever know what happened aboard the *Star Queen*.

In any case, McNeil probably cared nothing for the world's opinion, thanks to the sleek self-sufficiency that had so often annoyed Grant. But that very self-sufficiency meant that at all costs he must preserve his own good opinion of himself. Without it life would not be worth living—and McNeil had never accepted life save on his own terms.

The engineer was watching him intently and must have guessed that Grant was coming near the truth, for he suddenly changed his tone as though he was sorry he had revealed so much of his character.

"Don't think I get a quixotic pleasure from turning the other cheek," he said. "Just consider it from the point of view of pure logic. After all, we've got to come to *some* agreement.

"Has it occurred to you that if only one of us survives without a covering message from the other, he'll have a very uncomfortable time explaining just what happened?"

In his blind fury, Grant had completely forgotten this. But he did not believe it bulked at all important in McNeil's own thoughts.

"Yes," he said, "I suppose you're right."

He felt far better now. All the hate had drained out of him and he was at peace. The truth was known and he accepted it. That it was so different from what he had imagined did not seem to matter now.

"Well, let's get it over," he said unemotionally. "There's a new pack of cards lying around somewhere."

"I think we'd better speak to Venus first—both of us," replied McNeil, with peculiar emphasis. "We want a complete agreement on record in case anyone asks awkward questions later."

Grant nodded absently. He did not mind very much now one way or the other. He even smiled, ten minutes later, as he drew his card from the pack and laid it, face upward, beside McNeil's.

"So that's the whole story, is it?" said the first mate, wondering how soon he could decently get to the transmitter.

"Yes," said McNeil evenly, "that's all there was to it."

The mate bit his pencil, trying to frame the next question. "And I suppose Grant took it all quite calmly?"

The captain gave him a glare, which he avoided, and McNeil looked at him coldly as if he could see through to the sensation-mongering headlines ranged behind. He got to his feet and moved over to the observation port.

"You heard his broadcast, didn't you? Wasn't that calm enough?"

The mate sighed. It still seemed hard to believe that in such circumstances two men could have behaved in so reasonable, so unemotional a manner. He could have pictured all sorts of dramatic possibilities—sudden outbursts of insanity, even attempts at murder. Yet according to McNeil nothing at all had happened. It was too bad.

McNeil was speaking again, as if to himself. "Yes, Grant behaved very well—very well indeed. It was a great pity—"

Then he seemed to lose himself in the ever-fresh, incomparable glory of the approaching planet. Not far beneath, and coming closer by kilometers every second, the snow-white crescent arms of Venus spanned more than half the sky. Down there were life and warmth and civilization—and air.

The future, which not long ago had seemed contracted to a point, had opened out again into all its unknown possibilities and wonders. But behind him McNeil could sense the eyes of his rescuers, probing, questioning—yes, and condemning too.

All his life he would hear whispers. Voices would be saying behind his back, "Isn't that the man who—?"

He did not care. For once in his life at least, he had done something of which he could feel unashamed. Perhaps one day his own pitiless self-analysis would strip bare the motives behind his actions, would whisper in his ear. "Altruism? Don't be a fool! You did it to bolster up your own good opinion of yourself—so much more important than anyone else's!"

But the perverse maddening voices, which all his life had made nothing seem worthwhile, were silent for the moment and he felt content. He had reached the calm at the center of the hurricane. While it lasted he would enjoy it to the full.

History Lesson

No one could remember when the tribe had begun its long journey. The land of great rolling plains that had been its first home was now no more than a half-forgotten dream.

For many years Shann and his people had been fleeing through a country of low hills and sparkling lakes, and now the mountains lay ahead. This summer they must cross them to the southern lands. There was little time to lose. The white terror that had come down from the Poles, grinding continents to dust and freezing the very air before it, was less than a day's march behind.

Shann wondered if the glaciers could climb the mountains ahead, and within his heart he dared to kindle a little flame of hope. This might prove a barrier against which even the remorseless ice would batter in vain. In the southern lands of which the legends spoke, his people might find refuge at last.

It took weeks to discover a pass through which the tribe and the animals could travel. When midsummer came, they had camped in a lonely valley where the air was thin and the stars shone with a brilliance no one had ever seen before.

The summer was waning when Shann took his two sons and went ahead to explore the way. For three days they climbed, and for three nights slept as best they could

73

on the freezing rocks, and on the fourth morning there
was nothing ahead but a gentle rise to a cairn of gray
stones built by other travelers, centuries ago.

Shann felt himself trembling, and not with cold, as they
walked toward the little pyramid of stones. His sons had
fallen behind. No one spoke, for too much was at stake.
In a little while they would know if all their hopes had
been betrayed.

To east and west, the wall of mountains curved away
as if embracing the land beneath. Below lay endless miles
of undulating plain, with a great river swinging across
it in tremendous loops. It was a fertile land; one in which
the tribe could raise crops knowing that there would be
no need to flee before the harvest came.

Then Shann lifted his eyes to the south, and saw the
doom of all his hopes. For there at the edge of the world
glimmered that deadly light he had seen so often to the
north—the glint of ice below the horizon.

There was no way forward. Through all the years of
flight, the glaciers from the south had been advancing
to meet them. Soon they would be crushed beneath the
moving walls of ice . . .

Southern glaciers did not reach the mountains until a
generation later. In that last summer the sons of Shann
carried the sacred treasures of the tribe to the lonely cairn
overlooking the plain. The ice that had once gleamed below the horizon was now almost at their feet. By spring
it would be splintering against the mountain walls.

No one understood the treasures now. They were from
a past too distant for the understanding of any man alive.
Their origins were lost in the mists that surrounded the
Golden Age, and how they had come at last into the possession of this wandering tribe was a story that now
would never be told. For it was the story of a civilization
that had passed beyond recall.

Once, all these pitiful relics had been treasured for
some good reason, and now they had become sacred
though their meaning had long been lost. The print in
the old books had faded centuries ago though much of

the lettering was still visible—if there had been any to read it. But many generations had passed since anyone had had a use for a set of seven-figure logarithms, an atlas of the world, and the score of Sibelius' Seventh Symphony printed, according to the flyleaf, by H. K. Chu and Sons, at the City of Pekin in the year 2371 A.D.

The old books were placed reverently in the little crypt that had been made to receive them. There followed a motley collection of fragments—gold and platinum coins, a broken telephoto lens, a watch, a cold-light lamp, a microphone, the cutter from an electric razor, some midget radio tubes, the flotsam that had been left behind when the great tide of civilization had ebbed forever.

All these treasures were carefully stowed away in their resting place. Then came three more relics, the most sacred of all because the least understood.

The first was a strangely shaped piece of metal, showing the coloration of intense heat. It was, in its way, the most pathetic of all these symbols from the past, for it told of man's greatest achievement and of the future he might have known. The mahogany stand on which it was mounted bore a silver plate with the inscription.

Auxiliary Igniter from Starboard Jet
Spaceship "Morning Star"
Earth-Moon, A.D. 1985

Next followed another miracle of the ancient science— a sphere of transparent plastic with strangely shaped pieces of metal imbedded in it. At its center was a tiny capsule of synthetic radio-element, surrounded by the converting screens that shifted its radiation far down the spectrum. As long as the material remained active, the sphere would be a tiny radio transmitter, broadcasting power in all directions. Only a few of these spheres had ever been made. They had been designed as perpetual beacons to mark the orbits of the asteroids. But man had never reached the asteroids and the beacons had never been used.

Last of all was a flat, circular tin, wide in comparison

with its depth. It was heavily sealed, and rattled when shaken. The tribal lore predicted that disaster would follow if it was ever opened, and no one knew that it held one of the great works of art of nearly a thousand years before.

The work was finished. The two men rolled the stones back into place and slowly began to descend the mountainside. Even to the last, man had given some thought to the future and had tried to preserve something for posterity.

That winter the great waves of ice began their first assault on the mountains, attacking from north and south. The foothills were overwhelmed in the first onslaught, and the glaciers ground them into dust. But the mountains stood firm, and when the summer came the ice retreated for a while.

So, winter after winter, the battle continued, and the roar of the avalanches, the grinding of rock and the explosions of splintering ice filled the air with tumult. No war of man's had been fiercer than this, and even man's battles had not quite engulfed the globe as this had done.

At last the tidal waves of ice began to subside and to creep slowly down the flanks of the mountains they had never quite subdued. The valleys and passes were still firmly in their grip. It was stalemate. The glaciers had met their match, but their defeat was too late to be of any use to man.

So the centuries passed, and presently there happened something that must occur once at least in the history of every world in the universe, no matter how remote and lonely it may be.

The ship from Venus came five thousand years too late, but its crew knew nothing of this. While still many millions of miles away, the telescopes had seen the great shroud of ice that made Earth the most brilliant object in the sky next to the sun itself.

Here and there the dazzling sheet was marred by black specks that revealed the presence of almost buried mountains. That was all. The rolling oceans, the plains and forests, the deserts and lakes—all that had been the world of man was sealed beneath the ice, perhaps forever.

The ship closed in to Earth and established an orbit less than a thousand miles away. For five days it circled the planet, while cameras recorded all that was left to see and a hundred instruments gathered information that would give the Venusian scientists many years of work.

An actual landing was not intended. There seemed little purpose in it. But on the sixth day the picture changed. A panoramic monitor, driven to the limit of its amplification, detected the dying radiation of the five-thousand-year-old beacon. Through all the centuries, it had been sending out its signals with ever-failing strength as its radioactive heart steadily weakened.

The monitor locked on the beacon frequency. In the control room, a bell clamored for attention. A little later, the Venusian ship broke free from its orbit and slanted down toward Earth, toward a range of mountains that still towered proudly above the ice, and to a cairn of gray stones that the years had scarcely touched. . . .

The great disk of the sun blazed fiercely in a sky no longer veiled with mist, for the clouds that had once hidden Venus had now completely gone. Whatever force had caused the change in the sun's radiation had doomed one civilization, but had given birth to another. Less than five thousand years before, the half-savage people of Venus had seen sun and stars for the first time. Just as the science of Earth had begun with astronomy, so had that of Venus, and on the warm, rich world that man had never seen progress had been incredibly rapid.

Perhaps the Venusians had been lucky. They never knew the Dark Age that held man enchained for a thousand years. They missed the long detour into chemistry and mechanics but came at once to the more fundamental laws of radiation physics. In the time that man had taken to progress from the Pyramids to the rocket-propelled spaceship, the Venusians had passed from the discovery of agriculture to antigravity itself—the ultimate secret that man had never learned.

The warm ocean that still bore most of the young planet's life rolled its breakers languidly against the sandy shore. So new was this continent that the very sands were coarse and gritty. There had not yet been time enough for the sea to wear them smooth.

The scientists lay half in the water, their beautiful reptilian bodies gleaming in the sunlight. The greatest minds of Venus had gathered on this shore from all the islands of the planet. What they were going to hear they did not know, except that it concerned the Third World and the mysterious race that had peopled it before the coming of the ice.

The Historian was standing on the land, for the instruments he wished to use had no love of water. By his side was a large machine which attracted many curious glances from his colleagues. It was clearly concerned with optics, for a lens system projected from it toward a screen of white material a dozen yards away.

The Historian began to speak. Briefly he recapitulated what little had been discovered concerning the Third Planet and its people,

He mentioned the centuries of fruitless research that had failed to interpret a single word of the writings of Earth. The planet had been inhabited by a race of great technical ability. That, at least, was proved by the few pieces of machinery that had been found in the cairn upon the mountain.

"We do not know why so advanced a civilization came to an end," he observed. "Almost certainly, it had sufficient knowledge to survive an Ice Age. There must have been some other factor of which we know nothing. Possibly disease or racial degeneration may have been responsible. It has even been suggested that the tribal conflicts endemic to our own species in prehistoric times may have continued on the Third Planet after the coming of technology.

"Some philosophers maintain that knowledge of machinery does not necessarily imply a high degree of civilization, and it is theoretically possible to have wars in a society possessing mechanical power, flight, and even radio. Such a conception is alien to our thoughts, but we must admit its possibility. It would certainly account for the downfall of the lost race.

"It has always been assumed that we should never know anything of the physical form of the creatures who lived on Planet Three. For centuries our artists have been depicting scenes from the history of the dead world, peopling it with all manner of fantastic beings. Most of these creations have resembled us more or less closely, though it has often been pointed out that because *we* are reptiles it does not follow that all intelligent life must necessarily be reptilian.

"We now know the answer to one of the most baffling problems of history. At last, after hundreds of years of research, we have discovered the exact form and nature of the ruling life on the Third Planet."

There was a murmur of astonishment from the assembled scientists. Some were so taken aback that they disappeared for a while into the comfort of the ocean, as all Venusians were apt to do in moments of stress. The Historian waited until his colleagues re-emerged into the element they so disliked. He himself was quite comfortable, thanks to the tiny sprays that were continually playing over his body. With their help he could live on land for many hours before having to return to the ocean.

The excitement slowly subsided and the lecturer continued:

"One of the most puzzling of the objects found on Planet Three was a flat metal container holding a great length of transparent plastic material, perforated at the edges and wound tightly into a spool. This transparent tape at first seemed quite featureless, but an examination with the new subelectronic microscope has shown that this is not the case. Along the surface of the material, invisible to our eyes but perfectly clear under the correct radiation, are literally thousands of tiny pictures. It is believed that they were imprinted on the material by some chemical means, and have faded with the passage of time.

"These pictures apparently form a record of life as it

was on the Third Planet at the height of its civilization.
They are not independent. Consecutive pictures are almost identical, differing only in the detail of movement.
The purpose of such a record is obvious. It is only necessary to project the scenes in rapid succession to give an
illusion of continuous movement. We have made a machine to do this, and I have here an exact reproduction
of the picture sequence.

"The scenes you are now going to witness take us back
many thousands of years, to the great days of our sister
planet. They show a complex civilization, many of whose
activities we can only dimly understand. Life seems to
have been very violent and energetic, and much that you
will see is quite baffling.

"It is clear that the Third Planet was inhabited by a
number of different species, none of them reptilian. That
is a blow to our pride, but the conclusion is inescapable.
The dominant type of life appears to have been a two-
armed biped. It walked upright and covered its body
with some flexible material, possibly for protection
against the cold, since even before the Ice Age the planet
was at a much lower temperature than our own world.
But I will not try your patience any further. You will
now see the record of which I have been speaking."

A brilliant light flashed from the projector. There was
a gentle whirring, and on the screen appeared hundreds
of strange beings moving rather jerkily to and fro. The
picture expanded to embrace one of the creatures, and
the scientists could see that the Historian's description
had been correct.

The creature possessed two eyes, set rather close together, but the other facial adornments were a little obscure. There was a large orifice in the lower portion of
the head that was continually opening and closing. Possibly it had something to do with the creature's breathing.

The scientists watched spellbound as the strange being
became involved in a series of fantastic adventures. There
was an incredibly violent conflict with another, slightly
different creature. It seemed certain that they must both

be killed, but when it was all over neither seemed any the worse.

Then came a furious drive over miles of country in a four-wheeled mechanical device which was capable of extraordinary feats of locomotion. The ride ended in a city packed with other vehicles moving in all directions at breathtaking speeds. No one was surprised to see two of the machines meet head-on with devastating results.

After that, events became even more complicated. It was now quite obvious that it would take many years of research to analyze and understand all that was happening. It was also clear that the record was a work of art, somewhat stylized, rather than an exact reproduction of life as it actually had been on the Third Planet.

Most of the scientists felt themselves completely dazed when the sequence of pictures came to an end. There was a final flurry of motion, in which the creature that had been the center of interest became involved in some tremendous but incomprehensible catastrophe. The picture contracted to a circle, centered on the creature's head.

The last scene of all was an expanded view of its face, obviously expressing some powerful emotion. But whether it was rage, grief, defiance, resignation or some other feeling could not be guessed. The picture vanished. For a moment some lettering appeared on the screen, then it was all over.

For several minutes there was complete silence, save for the lapping of the waves upon the sand. The scientists were too stunned to speak. The fleeting glimpse of Earth's civilization had had a shattering effect on their minds. Then little groups began to start talking together, first in whispers and then more and more loudly as the implications of what they had seen became clearer. Presently the Historian called for attention and addressed the meeting again.

"We are now planning," he said, "a vast program of research to extract all available knowledge from this record. Thousands of copies are being made for distribution to all workers. You will appreciate the problems involved.

The psychologists in particular have an immense task confronting them.

"But I do not doubt that we shall succeed. In another generation, who can say what we may not have learned of this wonderful race? Before we leave, let us look again at our remote cousins, whose wisdom may have surpassed our own but of whom so little has survived."

Once more the final picture flashed on the screen, motionless this time, for the projector had been stopped. With something like awe, the scientists gazed at the still figure from the past, while in turn the little biped stared back at them with its characteristic expression of arrogant bad temper.

For the rest of time it would symbolize the human race. The psychologists of Venus would analyze its actions and watch its every movement until they could reconstruct its mind. Thousands of books would be written about it. Intricate philosophies would be contrived to account for its behavior.

But all this labor, all this research, would be utterly in vain. Perhaps the proud and lonely figure on the screen was smiling sardonically at the scientists who were starting on their age-long fruitless quest.

Its secret would be safe as long as the universe endured, for no one now would ever read the lost language of Earth. Millions of times in the ages to come those last few words would flash across the screen, and none could ever guess their meaning:

A Walt Disney Production.

Superiority

In making this statement—which I do of my own free will—I wish first to make it perfectly clear that I am not in any way trying to gain sympathy, nor do I expect any mitigation of whatever sentence the Court may pronounce. I am writing this in an attempt to refute some of the lying reports broadcast over the prison radio and published in the papers I have been allowed to see. These have given an entirely false picture of the true cause of our defeat, and as the leader of my race's armed forces at the cessation of hostilities I feel it my duty to protest against such libels upon those who served under me.

I also hope that this statement may explain the reasons for the application I have twice made to the Court, and will now induce it to grant a favor for which I can see no possible grounds of refusal.

The ultimate cause of our failure was a simple one: despite all statements to the contrary, it was not due to lack of bravery on the part of our men, or to any fault of the Fleet's. We were defeated by one thing only —by the inferior science of our enemies. I repeat—by the *inferior* science of our enemies.

When the war opened we had no doubt of our ultimate victory. The combined fleets of our allies greatly exceeded in number and armament those which the en-

emy could muster against us, and in almost all branches
of military science we were their superiors. We were
sure that we could maintain this superiority. Our belief
proved, alas, to be only too well founded.

At the opening of the war our main weapons were the
long-range homing torpedo, dirigible ball-lightning and
the various modifications of the Klydon beam. Every
unit of the Fleet was equipped with these and though
the enemy possessed similar weapons their installations
were generally of lesser power. Moreover, we had behind us a far greater military Research Organization,
and with this initial advantage we could not possibly
lose.

The campaign proceeded according to plan until the
Battle of the Five Suns. We won this, of course, but the
opposition proved stronger than we had expected. It was
realized that victory might be more difficult, and more
delayed, than had first been imagined. A conference of
supreme commanders was therefore called to discuss our
future strategy.

Present for the first time at one of our war conferences was Professor-General Norden, the new Chief of
the Research Staff, who had just been appointed to fill
the gap left by the death of Malvar, our greatest scientist. Malvar's leadership had been responsible, more
than any other single factor, for the efficiency and power
of our weapons. His loss was a very serious blow, but no
one doubted the brilliance of his successor—though
many of us disputed the wisdom of appointing a theoretical scientist to fill a post of such vital importance.
But we had been overruled.

I can well remember the impression Norden made at
that conference. The military advisers were worried, and
as usual turned to the scientists for help. Would it be
possible to improve our existing weapons, they asked, so
that our present advantage could be increased still further?

Norden's reply was quite unexpected. Malvar had often been asked such a question—and he had always done
what we requested.

"Frankly, gentlemen," said Norden, "I doubt it. Our existing weapons have practically reached finality. I don't wish to criticize my predecessor, or the excellent work done by the Research Staff in the last few generations, but do you realize that there has been no basic change in armaments for over a century? It is, I am afraid, the result of a tradition that has become conservative. For too long, the Research Staff has devoted itself to perfecting old weapons instead of developing new ones. It is fortunate for us that our opponents have been no wiser: we cannot assume that this will always be so."

Norden's words left an uncomfortable impression, as he had no doubt intended. He quickly pressed home the attack.

"What we want are *new* weapons—weapons totally different from any that have been employed before. Such weapons can be made: it will take time, of course, but since assuming charge I have replaced some of the older scientists by young men and have directed research into several unexplored fields which show great promise. I believe, in fact, that a revolution in warfare may soon be upon us."

We were skeptical. There was a bombastic tone in Norden's voice that made us suspicious of his claims. We did not know, then, that he never promised anything that he had not already almost perfected in the laboratory. *In the laboratory*—that was the operative phrase.

Norden proved his case less than a month later, when he demonstrated the Sphere of Annihilation, which produced complete disintegration of matter over a radius of several hundred meters. We were intoxicated by the power of the new weapon, and were quite prepared to overlook one fundamental defect—the fact that it *was* a sphere and hence destroyed its rather complicated generating equipment at the instant of formation. This meant, of course, that it could not be used on warships but only on guided missiles, and a great program was started to convert all homing torpedoes to carry the new weapon. For the time being all further offensives were suspended.

We realize now that this was our first mistake. I still think that it was a natural one, for it seemed to us then that all our existing weapons had become obsolete overnight, and we already regarded them as almost primitive survivals. What we did not appreciate was the magnitude of the task we were attempting, and the length of time it would take to get the revolutionary super-weapon into battle. Nothing like this had happened for a hundred years and we had no previous experience to guide us.

The conversion problem proved far more difficult than anticipated. A new class of torpedo had to be designed, as the standard model was too small. This meant in turn that only the larger ships could launch the weapon, but we were prepared to accept this penalty. After six months, the heavy units of the Fleet were being equipped with the Sphere. Training maneuvers and tests had shown that it was operating satisfactorily and we were ready to take it into action. Norden was already being hailed as the architect of victory, and had half promised even more spectacular weapons.

Then two things happened. One of our battleships disappeared completely on a training flight, and an investigation showed that under certain conditions the ship's long-range radar could trigger the Sphere immediately it had been launched. The modification needed to overcome this defect was trivial, but it caused a delay of another month and was the source of much bad feeling between the naval staff and the scientists. We were ready for action again—when Norden announced that the radius of effectiveness of the Sphere had now been increased by ten, thus multiplying by a thousand the chances of destroying an enemy ship.

So the modifications started all over again, but everyone agreed that the delay would be worth it. Meanwhile, however, the enemy had been emboldened by the absence of further attacks and had made an unexpected onslaught. Our ships were short of torpedoes, since none had been coming from the factories, and were forced to retire. So we lost the systems of Kyrane and Floranus, and the planetary fortress of Rhamsandron.

It was an annoying but not a serious blow, for the re-captured systems had been unfriendly, and difficult to ad-minister. We had no doubt that we could restore the position in the near future, as soon as the new weapon became operational.

These hopes were only partially fulfilled. When we renewed our offensive, we had to do so with fewer of the Spheres of Annihilation than had been planned, and this was one reason for our limited success. The other reason was more serious.

While we had been equipping as many of our ships as we could with the irresistible weapon, the enemy had been building feverishly. His ships were of the old pat-tern with the old weapons—but they now outnumbered ours. When we went into action, we found that the num-bers ranged against us were often 100 per cent greater than expected, causing target confusion among the auto-matic weapons and resulting in higher losses than antici-pated. The enemy losses were higher still, for once a Sphere had reached its objective, destruction was cer-tain, but the balance had not swung as far in our favor as we had hoped.

Moreover, while the main fleets had been engaged, the enemy had launched a daring attack on the lightly held systems of Eriston, Duranus, Carmanidora and Pharani-don—recapturing them all. We were thus faced with a threat only fifty light-years from our home planets.

There was much recrimination at the next meeting of the supreme commanders. Most of the complaints were addressed to Norden—Grand Admiral Taxaris in particu-lar maintaining that thanks to our admittedly irresistible weapon we were now considerably worse off than before. We should, he claimed, have continued to build conven-tional ships, thus preventing the loss of our numerical superiority.

Norden was equally angry and called the naval staff ungrateful bunglers. But I could tell that he was worried —as indeed we all were—by the unexpected turn of events. He hinted that there might be a speedy way of remedying the situation.

We now know that Research had been working on the Battle Analyzer for many years, but at the time it came as a revelation to us and perhaps we were too easily swept off our feet. Norden's argument, also, was seductively convincing. What did it matter, he said, if the enemy had twice as many ships as we—if the efficiency of ours could be doubled or even trebled? For decades the limiting factor in warfare had been not mechanical but biological—it had become more and more difficult for any single mind, or group of minds, to cope with the rapidly changing complexities of battle in three-dimensional space. Norden's mathematicians had analyzed some of the classic engagements of the past, and had shown that even when we had been victorious we had often operated our units at much less than half of their theoretical efficiency.

The Battle Analyzer would change all this by replacing the operations staff with electronic calculators. The idea was not new, in theory, but until now it had been no more than a utopian dream. Many of us found it difficult to believe that it was still anything but a dream: after we had run through several very complex dummy battles, however, we were convinced.

It was decided to install the Analyzer in four of our heaviest ships, so that each of the main fleets could be equipped with one. At this stage, the trouble began—though we did not know it until later.

The Analyzer contained just short of a million vaccum tubes and needed a team of five hundred technicians to maintain and operate it. It was quite impossible to accommodate the extra staff aboard a battleship, so each of the four units had to be accompanied by a converted liner to carry the technicians not on duty. Installation was also a very slow and tedious business, but by gigantic efforts it was completed in six months.

Then, to our dismay, we were confronted by another crisis. Nearly five thousand highly skilled men had been selected to serve the Analyzers and had been given an intensive course at the Technical Training Schools. At the end of seven months, 10 per cent of them had had nervous breakdowns and only 40 per cent had qualified.

Once again, everyone started to blame everyone else. Norden, of course, said that the Research Staff could not be held responsible, and so incurred the enmity of the Personnel and Training Commands. It was finally decided that the only thing to do was to use two instead of four Analyzers and to bring the others into action as soon as men could be trained. There was little time to lose, for the enemy was still on the offensive and his morale was rising.

The first Analyzer fleet was ordered to recapture the system of Eriston. On the way, by one of the hazards of war, the liner carrying the technicians was struck by a roving mine. A warship would have survived, but the liner with its irreplaceable cargo was totally destroyed. So the operation had to be abandoned.

The other expedition was, at first, more successful. There was no doubt at all that the Analyzer fulfilled its designers' claims, and the enemy was heavily defeated in the first engagements. He withdrew, leaving us in possession of Saphran, Leucon and Hexanerax. But his Intelligence Staff must have noted the change in our tactics and the inexplicable presence of a liner in the heart of our battle-fleet. It must have noted, also, that our first fleet had been accompanied by a similar ship—and had withdrawn when it had been destroyed.

In the next engagement, the enemy used his superior numbers to launch an overwhelming attack on the Analyzer ship and its unarmed consort. The attack was made without regard to losses—both ships were, of course, very heavily protected—and it succeeded. The result was the virtual decapitation of the Fleet, since an effectual transfer to the old operational methods proved impossible. We disengaged under heavy fire, and so lost all our gains and also the systems of Lormyia, Ismarnus, Beronis, Alphanidon and Sideneus.

At this stage, Grand Admiral Taxaris expressed his

disapproval of Norden by committing suicide, and I assumed supreme command.

The situation was now both serious and infuriating. With stubborn conservatism and complete lack of imagination, the enemy continued to advance with his old-fashioned and inefficient but now vastly more numerous ships. It was galling to realize that if we had only continued building, without seeking new weapons, we would have been in a far more advantageous position. There were many acrimonious conferences at which Norden defended the scientists while everyone else blamed them for all that had happened. The difficulty was that Norden had proved every one of his claims: he had a perfect excuse for all the disasters that had occurred. And we could not now turn back—the search for an irresistible weapon must go on. At first it had been a luxury that would shorten the war. Now it was a necessity if we were to end it victoriously.

We were on the defensive, and so was Norden. He was more than ever determined to re-establish his prestige and that of the Research Staff. But we had been twice disappointed, and would not make the same mistake again. No doubt Norden's twenty thousand scientists would produce many further weapons: we would remain unimpressed.

We were wrong. The final weapon was something so fantastic that even now it seems difficult to believe that it ever existed. Its innocent, noncommittal name—The Exponential Field—gave no hint of its real potentialities. Some of Norden's mathematicians had discovered it during a piece of entirely theoretical research into the properties of space, and to everyone's great surprise their results were found to be physically realizable.

It seems very difficult to explain the operation of the Field to the layman. According to the technical description, it "produces an exponential condition of space, so that a finite distance in normal, linear space may become infinite in pseudo-space." Norden gave an analogy which some of us found useful. It was as if one took a flat disk of rubber—representing a region of normal space—and then pulled its center out to infinity. The circumference of the disk would be unaltered—but its "diameter" would be infinite. That was the sort of thing the generator of the Field did to the space around it.

As an example, suppose that a ship carrying the generator was surrounded by a ring of hostile machines. If it switched on the Field, *each* of the enemy ships would think that it—and the ships on the far side of the circle —had suddenly receded into nothingness. Yet the circumference of the circle would be the same as before: only the journey to the center would be of infinite duration, for as one proceeded, distances would appear to become greater and greater as the "scale" of space altered.

It was a nightmare condition, but a very useful one. Nothing could reach a ship carrying the Field: it might be englobed by an enemy fleet yet would be as inaccessible as if it were at the other side of the Universe. Against this, of course, it could not fight back without switching off the Field, but this still left it at a very great advantage, not only in defense but in offense. For a ship fitted with the Field could approach an enemy fleet undetected and suddenly appear in its midst.

This time there seemed to be no flaws in the new weapon. Needless to say, we looked for all the possible objections before we committed ourselves again. Fortunately the equipment was fairly simple and did not require a large operating staff. After much debate, we decided to rush it into production, for we realized that time was running short and the war was going against us. We had now lost about the whole of our initial gains and enemy forces had made several raids into our own solar system.

We managed to hold off the enemy while the Fleet was re-equipped and the new battle techniques were worked out. To use the Field operationally it was necessary to locate an enemy formation, set a course that would intercept it, and then switch on the generator for the calculated period of time. On releasing the Field again—if the calculations had been accurate—one would be in the enemy's midst and could do great dam-

age during the resulting confusion, retreating by the
same route when necessary.

The first trial maneuvers proved satisfactory and the
equipment seemed quite reliable. Numerous mock attacks were made and the crews became accustomed to
the new technique. I was on one of the test flights and
can vividly remember my impressions as the Field was
switched on. The ships around us seemed to dwindle as
if on the surface of an expanding bubble: in an instant
they had vanished completely. So had the stars—but
presently we could see that the Galaxy was still visible
as a faint band of light around the ship. The virtual
radius of our pseudo-space was not really infinite, but
some hundred thousand light-years, and so the distance
to the farthest stars of our system had not been greatly
increased—though the nearest had of course totally disappeared.

These training maneuvers, however, had to be can-
celled before they were complete owing to a whole flock
of minor technical troubles in various pieces of equipment, notably the communications circuits. These were
annoying, but not important, though it was thought best
to return to Base to clear them up.

At that moment the enemy made what was obviously
intended to be a decisive attack against the fortress
planet of Iton at the limits of our solar system. The Fleet
had to go into battle before repairs could be made.

The enemy must have believed that we had mastered
the secret of invisibility—as in a sense we had. Our ships
appeared suddenly out of nowhere and inflicted tremendous damage—for a while. And then something quite
baffling and inexplicable happened.

I was in command of the flagship *Hircania* when the
trouble started. We had been operating as independent
units, each against assigned objectives. Our detectors observed an enemy formation at medium range and the
navigating officers measured its distance with great ac-
curacy. We set course and switched on the generator.

The Exponential Field was released at the moment
when we should have been passing through the center

of the enemy group. To our consternation, we emerged into normal space at a distance of many hundred miles —and when we found the enemy, he had already found us. We retreated, and tried again. This time we were so far away from the enemy that he located us first.

Obviously, something was seriously wrong. We broke communicator silence and tried to contact the other ships of the Fleet to see if they had experienced the same trouble. Once again we failed—and this time the failure was beyond all reason, for the communication equipment appeared to be working perfectly. We could only assume, fantastic though it seemed, that the rest of the Fleet had been destroyed.

I do not wish to describe the scenes when the scattered units of the Fleet struggled back to Base. Our casualties had actually been negligible, but the ships were completely demoralized. Almost all had lost touch with one another and had found that their ranging equipment showed inexplicable errors. It was obvious that the Exponential Field was the cause of the troubles, despite the fact that they were only apparent when it was switched off.

The explanation came too late to do us any good, and Norden's final discomfiture was small consolation for the virtual loss of the war. As I have explained, the Field generators produced a radial distortion of space, distances appearing greater and greater as one approached the center of the artificial pseudo-space. When the Field was switched off, conditions returned to normal.

But not quite. It was never possible to restore the initial state *exactly*. Switching the Field on and off was equivalent to an elongation and contraction of the ship carrying the generator, but there was an hysteretic effect, as it were, and the initial condition was never quite reproducible, owing to all the thousands of electrical changes and movements of mass aboard the ship while the Field was on. These asymmetries and distortions were cumulative, and though they seldom amounted to more than a fraction of one per cent, that was quite enough. It meant that the precision ranging equipment and the tuned circuits in the communication apparatus were thrown completely out of adjustment. Any single ship could never detect the change—only when it compared its equipment with that of another vessel, or tried to communciate with it, could it tell what had happened.

It is impossible to describe the resultant chaos. Not a single component of one ship could be expected with certainty to work aboard another. The very nuts and bolts were no longer interchangeable, and the supply position became quite impossible. Given time, we might even have overcome these difficulties, but the enemy ships were already attacking in thousands with weapons which now seemed centuries behind those that we had invented. Our magnificent Fleet, crippled by our own science, fought on as best it could until it was overwhelmed and forced to surrender. The ships fitted with the Field were still invulnerable, but as fighting units they were almost helpless. Every time they switched on their generators to escape from enemy attack, the permanent distortion of their equipment increased. In a month, it was all over.

This is the true story of our defeat, which I give without prejudice to my defense before this Court. I make it, as I have said, to counteract the libels that have been circulating against the men who fought under me, and to show where the true blame for our misfortunes lay.

Finally, my request, which as the Court will now realize, I make in no frivolous manner and which I hope will therefore be granted.

The Court will be aware that the conditions under which we are housed and the constant surveillance to which we are subjected night and day are somewhat distressing. Yet I am not complaining of this: nor do I complain of the fact that shortage of accommodation has made it necessary to house us in pairs.

But I cannot be held responsible for my future actions if I am compelled any longer to share my cell with Professor Norden, late Chief of the Research Staff of my armed forces.

Exile of the Eons

Already the mountains were trembling with the thunder that only man can make. But here the war seemed very far away, for the full moon hung over The Himalayas and the blinding furies of the battle were still hidden below the edge of the world. Not for long would they remain. The Master knew that the last remnants of his fleet were being hurled from the sky as the circle of death closed swiftly on his stronghold.

In a few hours at the most, the Master and his dreams of empire would have vanished into the past. Nations would still curse his name, but they would no longer fear it. Later, even the hatred would be gone and he would mean no more to the world than Hitler or Napoleon or Genghis Khan. Like them he would be a blurred figure far down the infinite corridor of time, dwindling toward oblivion.

Far to the south, a mountain was suddenly edged with violet flame. Ages later, the balcony on which the Master stood shuddered beneath the impact of the ground wave racing through the rocks below. Later still, the air brought the echo to a mammoth concussion. Surely they could not be so close already! The Master hoped it was no more than a stray torpedo that had swept through the contracting battle line. If it were not, time was even shorter than he feared.

The Chief of Staff walked out from the shadows and joined him by the rail. The Marshal's hard face—the second most hated in all the world—was lined and beaded with sweat. He had not slept for many days and his once gaudy uniform hung limply upon him. Yet his eyes, though unutterably weary, were still resolute even in defeat. He stood in silence, awaiting his last orders. Nothing else was left for him to do.

Thirty miles away, the eternal snow-plume of Everest flamed a lurid red, reflecting the glare of some colossal fire below the horizon. Still the Master neither moved nor gave any sign. Not until a salvo of torpedoes passed high overhead with a demon wail did he turn and, with one backward glance at the world he would see no more, descend into the depths.

The lift dropped a thousand feet and the sound of battle died away. As he stepped out of the shaft, the Master paused for a moment to press a hidden switch. The Marshal smiled when he heard the crash of falling rock far above, and knew that pursuit and escape were equally impossible.

As of old, the handful of generals sprang to their feet when the Master entered the room. He walked to his place in silence, steeling himself for the last and hardest speech he would ever have to make. Burning into his soul he could feel the eyes of the men he had led to ruin. Behind and beyond them he could see the squadrons, the divisions, the armies whose blood was on his hands. And more terrible still were the silent specters of the nations that now could never be born.

At last he began to speak. The hypnosis of his voice was as powerful as ever, and after a few words he became once more the perfect, implacable machine whose destiny was destruction.

"This, gentlemen, is the last of all our meetings. There are no more plans to make, no more maps to study. Somewhere above our heads the fleet we built with such pride and care is fighting to the end. In a few minutes, not one of all those thousands of machines will be left in the sky.

"I know that for all of us here surrender is unthinkable, even if it were possible, so in this room you will shortly have to die. You have served our cause and deserved better, but it was not to be. Yet I do not wish you to think that we have wholly failed. In the past, as you saw many times, my plans were always ready for everything that might arise, no matter how improbable. You should not, therefore, be surprised to learn that I was prepared even for defeat."

Still the same superb orator, he paused for effect, noting with satisfaction the ripple of interest, the sudden alertness on the tired faces of his listeners.

"My secret is safe enough with you," he continued, "for the enemy will never find this place. The entrance is already blocked by many hundreds of feet of rock."

Still there was no movement. Only the Director of Propaganda turned suddenly white, and swiftly recovered—but not swiftly enough to escape the Master's eye. The Master smiled inwardly at this belated confirmation of an old doubt. It mattered little now; true and false, they would all die together.

All but one.

"Two years ago," he went on, "when we lost the battle of Antarctica, I knew that we could no longer be certain of victory. So I made my preparations for this day. The enemy has already sworn to kill me. I could not remain in hiding anywhere on the Earth, still less hope to rebuild our fortunes.

"But there is another way, though a desperate one.

"Five years ago, one of our scientists perfected the technique of suspended animation. He found that by relatively simple means all life processes could be arrested for an indefinite time. I am going to use this discovery to escape from the present into a future which will have forgotten me. There I can begin the struggle again, with the help of certain devices that might yet have won this war had we been granted more time.

"Good-by, gentlemen. And once again, my thanks for your help and my regrets at your ill fortune."

He saluted, turned on his heel, and was gone. The

metal door thudded decisively behind him. There was a frozen silence; then the Director of Propaganda rushed to the exit, only to recoil with a startled cry. The steel door was already too hot to touch. It had been welded immovably into the wall.

The Minister for War was the first to draw his automatic.

The Master was in no great hurry now. On leaving the council room he had thrown the secret switch of the welding circuit. The same action had opened a panel in the wall of the corridor, revealing a small circular passage sloping steadily upward. He began to walk slowly along it.

Every few hundred feet the tunnel angled sharply, though still continuing the upward climb. At each turning the Master stopped to throw a switch, and there was the thunder of falling rock as a section of corridor collapsed.

Five times the passageway changed its course before it ended in a spherical, metal-walled room. Multiple doors closed softly on rubber seatings, and the last section of tunnel crashed behind. The Master would not be disturbed by his enemies, nor by his friends.

He looked swiftly around the room to satisfy himself that all was ready. Then he walked to a simple control board and threw, one after another, a set of tiny switches. They had to carry little current—but they had been built to last. So had everything in that strange room. Even the walls were made of metals far less ephemeral than steel.

Pumps started to whine, drawing the air from the chamber and replacing it with sterile nitrogen. Moving more swiftly now, the Master went to the padded couch and lay down. He thought he could feel himself bathed by the bacteria-destroying rays from the lamps above his head, but that of course was fancy. From a recess beneath the couch he drew a hypodermic and injected a milky fluid into his arm.

Then he relaxed and waited.

It was already very cold. Soon the refrigerators would bring the temperature down far below freezing, and would hold it there for many hours. Then it would rise to normal, but by that time the process would be completed, all bacteria would be dead and the Master could sleep, unchanged, forever.

He had planned to wait a hundred years. More than that he dared not delay, for when he awoke he would have to master all the changes in science and society that the passing years had wrought. Even a century might have altered the face of a civilization beyond his understanding, but that was a risk he would have to take. Less than a century would not be safe, for the world would still be full of bitter memories.

Sealed in a vacuum beneath the couch were the electronic counters operated by thermocouples hundreds of feet above, on the eastern face of the mountain where no snow could ever cling. Every day the rising sun would operate them and the counters would add one unit to their store. So the coming of dawn would be noted in the darkness where the Master slept.

When any one of the counters reached the total of thirty-six thousand, a switch would close and oxygen would flow back into the chamber. The temperature would rise, and the automatic hypodermic strapped to the Master's arm would inject the calculated amount of fluid. He would awaken. Then he would press the button which would blast away the mountainside and give him free passage to the outer world.

Everything had been considered. There could be no failure. All the machinery had been triplicated and was as perfect as science could contrive.

The Master's last thought as consciousness ebbed was not of his past life, nor of the mother whose hopes he had betrayed. Unbidden and unwelcome, there came into his mind the words of an ancient poet:

To sleep, perchance to dream . . .

No, he would not, he dared not dream. He would only sleep . . . sleep . . . sleep. . .

Twenty miles away, the battle was coming to its end. Not a dozen of the Master's ships were left, fighting hopelessly against overwhelming fire. The action would have ended long ago had the attackers not been ordered to risk no ships in unnecessary adventures. The decision was to be left to the long-range artillery. So the great destroyers, the airborne battleships of this age, lay with their fighter screens in the shelter of the mountains, pouring salvo after salvo into the doomed formations.

Aboard the flagship, a young Hindu gunnery officer set vernier dials with infinite care and gently pressed a pedal with his foot. There was the faintest of shocks as the dirigible torpedoes left their cradles and hurled themselves at the enemy. The young Indian sat waiting tensely as the chronometer ticked off the seconds. This, he thought, was probably the last salvo he would ever fire. Somehow he felt none of the elation he had expected; indeed, he was surprised to discover a kind of impersonal sympathy for his doomed opponents, whose lives were now ebbing with every passing second.

Far away a sphere of violet fire blossomed above the mountains, among the darting specks that were enemy ships. The gunner leaned forward tensely and counted. One-two-three-four-five times came that peculiar explosion. Then the sky cleared. The struggling specks were gone.

In his log, the gunner noted briefly: "0124 hrs. Salvo No. 12 fired. Five torps exploded among enemy ships, which were destroyed. One torp failed to detonate."

He signed the entry with a flourish and laid down his pen. For a while he sat staring at the log's familiar brown cover, with the cigarette burns at the edges and the inevitable stained rings where cups and glasses had been carelessly set down. Idly he thumbed through the leaves, noting once again the handwriting of his many predecessors. And as he had done so often before, he turned to a familiar page where a man who had once been his

friend had begun to sign his name but had never lived
to complete it.

With a sigh, he closed the book and locked it away. The
war was over.

Far away among the mountains, the torpedo that had
failed to explode was still gaining speed under the drive of
its rockets. Now it was a scarcely visible line of light,
racing between the walls of a lonely valley. Already the
snows that had been disturbed by the scream of its
passage were beginning to rumble down the mountain
slopes.

There was no escape from the valley: it was blocked
by a sheer wall a thousand feet high. Here the torpedo
that had missed its mark found a greater one. The Master's tomb was too deep in the mountain even to be
shaken by the explosion but the hundreds of tons of falling rock swept away three tiny instruments and their con-
nections, and a future that might have been went with
them into oblivion.

The first rays of the rising sun would still fall on the
shattered face of the mountain, but the counters that
were waiting for the thirty-six thousandth dawn would
still be waiting when dawns and sunsets were no more.

In the silence of the tomb that was not quite a tomb,
the Master knew nothing of this. And he slumbered on,
until the century was far behind—very far indeed.

After what by some standards would have been a little while, the earth's crust decided it had borne the
weight of The Himalayas for long enough. Slowly the
mountains dropped, tilting the southern plains of India
toward the sky. And presently the plateau of Ceylon was
the highest point on the surface of the globe, and the
ocean about Everest was five and a half miles deep. Yet
the Master's slumber was still dreamless and undisturbed.

Slowly, patiently, the silt drifted down through the
towering ocean heights onto the wreck of The Himalayas.
The blanket that would one day be chalk began to
thicken at the rate of an inch or two every century. If

one had returned some time later, one might have found
that the sea bed was no longer five miles down, or even
four, or three. Then the land tilted again, and a mighty
range of limestone mountains towered where once had
been the oceans of Tibet. But the Master knew nothing
of this, nor was his sleep troubled when it happened
again and again and yet again.

Now the rain and the rivers were washing away the
chalk and carrying it out to the strange new oceans, and
the surface was moving down toward the hidden tomb.
Slowly the miles of rock were winnowed away until at
last the sphere which housed the Master's body returned
to the light of day—though to a day much longer, and
much dimmer, than it had been when the Master closed
his eyes.

Little did the Master dream of the races that had
flowered and died since that early morning of the world
when he went to his long sleep. Very far away was that
morning now, and the shadows were lengthening to the
east; the sun was dying and the world was very old. But
still the children of Adam ruled its seas and skies, and
filled with their tears and laughter the plains and the
valleys and the woods that were older than the shift-
ing hills.

The Master's dreamless sleep was more than half
ended when Trevindor the Philosopher was born, between the fall of the Ninety-seventh Dynasty and the
rise of the Fifth Galactic Empire. He was born on a
world very far from Earth. Few were the men who now
set foot on the ancient home of their race, so distant
from the throbbing heart of the Universe.

They brought Trevindor to Earth when his brief clash
with the Empire had come to its inevitable end. Here he
was tried by the men whose ideals he had challenged,
and here it was that they pondered long over the manner of his necessary fate.

The case was unique. The gentle, philosophic culture
that now ruled the Galaxy had never before met with
opposition, even on the level of pure intellect, and the
polite but implacable conflict of wills had left it severe-

ly shaken. It was typical of the Council's members that, when a decision had proved impossible, they had appealed to Trevindor himself for help.

In the whitely gleaming Hall of Justice, that had not been entered for nigh on a million years, Trevindor stood proudly facing the men who had proved stronger than he. In silence he listened to their request; then he paused in reflection. His judges waited patiently until at last he spoke.

"You suggest that I should promise not to defy you again," he began, "but I shall make no promise that I may be unable to keep. Our views are too divergent and sooner or later we should clash again.

"There was a time when your choice would have been easy. You could have exiled me, or put me to death. But today—where among all the worlds of the Universe is there one planet where you could hide me if I did not choose to stay? Remember, I have many disciples scattered the length and breadth of the Galaxy.

"There remains the other alternative. I shall bear you no malice if you revive the ancient custom of execution to meet my case."

There was a murmur of annoyance from the Council, and the President replied sharply, his color heightening.

"That remark is in questionable taste. We asked for serious suggestions, not reminders—even if intended humorously—of the barbaric customs of our remote ancestors."

Trevindor accepted the rebuke with a bow. "I was merely mentioning all the possibilities. There are two others that have occurred to me. It would be a simple matter to change my mind pattern to your way of thinking so that no future disagreement can arise."

"We have already considered that. We were forced to reject it, attractive though it is, for the destruction of your personality would be equivalent to murder. There are only fifteen more powerful intellects than yours in the Universe, and we have no right to tamper with it. And your final suggestion?"

"Though you cannot exile me in space, there is still

one alternative. The river of Time stretches ahead of us as far as our thoughts can go. Send me down that stream to an age when you are certain this civilization will have passed. That I know you can do with the aid of the Roston time-field."

There was a long pause. In silence the members of the Council were passing their decisions to the complex analysis machine which would weigh them one against the other and arrive at the verdict. At length the President spoke.

"It is agreed. We will send you to an age when the sun is still warm enough for life to exist on the Earth, but so remote that any trace of our civilization is unlikely to survive. We will also provide you with everything necessary for your safety and reasonable comfort. You may leave us now. We will call for you again as soon as all arrangements have been made."

Trevindor bowed, and left the marble hall. No guards followed him. There was nowhere he could flee, even if he wished, in this Universe which the great Galactic liners could span in a single day.

For the first and the last time, Trevindor stood on the shore of what had once been the Pacific, listening to the wind sighing through the leaves of what had once been palms. The few stars of the nearly empty region of space through which the sun was now passing shone with a steady light through the dry air of the aging world. Trevindor wondered bleakly if they would still be shining when he looked again upon the sky, in a future so distant that the sun itself would be sinking to its death.

There was a tinkle from the tiny communicator band upon his wrist. So, the time had come. He turned his back upon the ocean and walked resolutely to meet his fate. Before he had gone a dozen steps, the time-field had seized him and his thoughts froze in an instant that would remain unchanged while the oceans shrank and vanished, the Galactic Empire passed away, and the great star clusters crumbled into nothingness.

But, to Trevindor, no time elapsed at all. He only

knew that at one step there had been moist sand beneath his feet, and at the next hard, baked rock. The palms had vanished, the murmur of the sea was stilled. It needed only a glance to show that even the memory of the sea had long since faded from this parched and dying world. To the far horizon, a great desert of red sandstone stretched unbroken and unrelieved by any growing thing. Overhead, the orange disk of a strangely altered sun glowered from a sky so black that many stars were clearly visible.

Yet, it seemed, there was still life on this ancient world. To the north—if that were still the north—the somber light glinted upon some metallic structure. It was a few hundred yards away, and as Trevindor started to walk toward it he was conscious of a curious lightness, as if gravity itself had weakened.

He had not gone far before he saw that he was approaching a low metal building which seemed to have been set down on the plain rather than constructed there, for it tilted slightly with the slope of the land. Trevindor wondered at his incredible good fortune at finding civilization so easily. Another dozen steps, and he realized that not chance but design had so conveniently placed this building here, and that it was as much a stranger to this world as he himself.

There was no hope at all that anyone would come to meet him as he walked toward it.

The metal plaque above the door added little to what he had already surmised. Still new and untarnished as if it had just been engraved—as indeed, in a sense, it had—the lettering brought a message at once of hope and of bitterness.

To Trevindor, the greetings of the Council.

This building, which we have sent after you through the time-field, will supply all your needs for an indefinite period.

We do not know if civilization will still exist in the age in which you find yourself. Man may now be extinct, since the chromosome K Star K will have become dominant and the race may have mutated into something no longer human. That is for you to discover.

You are now in the twilight of the Earth and it is our hope that you are not alone. But if it is your destiny to be the last living creature on this once lovely world, remember that the choice was yours. Farewell.

Twice Trevindor read the message, recognizing with an ache the closing words which could only have been written by his friend, the poet Cintillarne. An overwhelming sense of loneliness and isolation came flooding into his soul. He sat down upon a shelf of rock and buried his face in his hands.

A long time later, he arose to enter the building. He felt more than grateful to the long-dead Council which had treated him so chivalrously. The technical achievement of sending an entire building through time was one he had believed beyond the resources of his age. A sudden thought struck him and he glanced again at the engraved lettering, noticing for the first time the date it bore. It was five thousand years later than the time when he had faced his peers in the Hall of Justice.

Fifty centuries had passed before his judges could redeem their promise to a man as good as dead. Whatever the faults of the Council, its integrity was of an order beyond the comprehension of an earlier age.

Many days passed before Trevindor left the building again. Nothing had been overlooked: even his beloved thought records were there. He could continue to study the nature of reality and to construct philosophies until the end of the Universe, barren though that occupation would be if his were the only mind left on Earth. There was little danger, he thought wryly, that his speculations concerning the purpose of human existence would once again bring him into conflict with society.

Not until he had investigated the building thoroughly did Trevindor turn his attention once more to the outer world. The supreme problem was that of contacting civilization, should such still exist. He had been provided with a powerful receiver, and for hours he wandered up and down the spectrum in the hope of discovering a station. The far-off crackle of static came from the instrument and once there was a burst of what might have been speech in a tongue that was certainly not human. But nothing else rewarded his search. The ether, which had been man's faithful servant for so many ages, was silent at last.

The little automatic flyer was Trevindor's sole remaining hope. He had what was left of eternity before him, and Earth was a small planet. In a few years at the most, he could have explored it all.

So the months passed while the exile began his methodical exploration of the world, returning ever and again to his home in the desert of red sandstone.

Everywhere he found the same picture of desolation and ruin. How long ago the seas had vanished he could not even guess, but in their dying they had left endless wastes of salt, encrusting both plains and mountains with a blanket of dirty gray.

Trevindor felt glad that he had not been born on Earth and so had never known it in the glory of its youth. Stranger though he was, the loneliness and desolation of the world chilled his heart; had he lived here before, its sadness would have been unbearable.

Thousands of square miles of desert passed beneath Trevindor's fleeting ship as he searched the world from pole to pole. Only once did he find any sign that Earth had ever known civilization. In a deep valley near the equator he discovered the ruins of a small city of strange white stone and stranger architecture. The buildings were perfectly preserved, though half buried by the drifting sand, and for a moment Trevindor felt a surge of somber joy at the knowledge that man had, after all, left some traces of his handiwork on the world that had been his first home.

The emotion was short-lived. The buildings were stranger than Trevindor had realized, for no man could ever have entered them. Their only openings were wide, horizontal slots close to the ground; there were no windows of any kind. Trevindor's mind reeled as he tried to imagine the creatures that must have occupied them. In spite of his growing loneliness, he felt glad that the dwellers in this inhuman city had passed away so long before his time. He did not linger here, for the bitter night was almost upon him and the valley filled him with an oppression that was not entirely rational.

And once, he actually discovered life. He was cruising over the bed of one of the lost oceans when a flash of color caught his eye. Upon a knoll which the drifting sand had not yet buried was a thin, wiry covering of grass. That was all, but the sight brought tears to his eyes.

He grounded the machine and stepped out, treading warily lest he destroy even one of the struggling blades. Tenderly he ran his hands over the threadbare carpet which was all the life that Earth now knew. Before he left, he sprinkled the spot with as much water as he could spare. It was a futile gesture, but one which made him feel happier.

The search was now nearly completed. Trevindor had long ago given up all hope, but his indomitable spirit still drove him on across the face of the world. He could not rest until he had proved what as yet he only feared. And thus it was that he came at last to the Master's tomb as it lay gleaming dully in the sunlight from which it had been banished so unthinkably long.

The Master's mind awoke before his body. As he lay powerless, unable even to lift his eyelids, memory came flooding back. The hundred years were safely behind him. His gamble, the most desperate that any man had ever made, had succeeded! An immense weariness came over him and for a while consciousness faded once more.

Presently the mists cleared again and he felt stronger, though still too weak to move. He lay in the darkness gathering his strength together. What sort of a world, he wondered, would he find when he stepped forth from the mountainside into the light of day? Would he be able to put his plans into—? What was that? A spasm of sheer terror shook the very foundations of his mind. Something was moving beside him, here in the tomb where nothing should be stirring but himself.

Then, calm and clear, a thought rang through his mind and quelled in an instant the fears that had threatened to overturn it.

"Do not be alarmed. I have come to help you. You are safe, and everything will be well."

The Master was too stunned to make any reply, but his subconscious must have formulated some sort of answer, for the thought came again.

"That is good. I am Trevindor, like yourself an exile in this world. Do not move, but tell me how you came here and what is your race, for I have seen none like it."

And now fear and caution were creeping back into the Master's mind. What manner of creature was this that could read his thoughts, and what was it doing in his secret sphere? Again that clear, cold thought echoed through his brain like the tolling of a bell.

"Once more I tell you that you have nothing to fear. Why are you alarmed because I can see into your mind? Surely there is nothing strange in that."

"Nothing strange!" cried the Master. "Who are you—what are you, for God's sake?"

"A man like yourself. But your race must be primitive indeed if the reading of thoughts is foreign to you."

A terrible suspicion began to dawn in the Master's brain. The answer came even before he consciously framed the question.

"You have slept infinitely longer than a hundred years. The world you knew has ceased to be for longer than you can imagine."

The Master heard no more. Once again the darkness swept over him and he sank down into unconsciousness.

In silence Trevindor stood by the couch on which the Master lay. He was filled with an elation which for the moment outweighed any disappointment he might feel. At least, he would no longer have to face the future alone. All the terror of the Earth's loneliness, that was weighing so heavily upon his soul, had vanished in a moment. *No longer alone* . . . no longer alone!

The Master was beginning to stir once more, and into Trevindor's mind crept broken fragments of thought. Pictures of the world the Master had known began to form. At first Trevindor could make nothing of them; then, suddenly, the jumbled shards fell into place. A wave of horror swept over him at the appalling vista of nation battling against nation, of cities flaming to destruction. What kind of world was this? Could man have sunk so low from the peaceful age Trevindor had known? There had been legends of such things, from times incredibly remote, but man had left them with his childhood. Surely they could never have returned!

The broken thoughts were more vivid now, and even more horrible. It was truly a nightmare age from which this other exile had come—no wonder that he had fled from it!

Suddenly the truth began to dawn in the mind of Trevindor as, sick at heart, he watched the ghastly patterns passing through the Master's brain. This was no exile seeking refuge from an age of horror. This was the very creator of that horror, who had embarked on the river of time with one purpose alone—to spread contagion down to later years.

Passions that Trevindor had never imagined began to parade themselves before his eyes: ambition, the lust for power, cruelty, intolerance, hatred. He tried to close his mind, but found he had lost the power to do so. With a cry of anguish, Trevindor rushed out into the silent desert.

It was night, and very still, for the Earth was now too weary even for winds to blow. The darkness hid everything, but Trevindor knew that it could not hide the thoughts of that other mind with which he now must share the world. Once he had been alone, and he had imagined nothing more dreadful. But now he knew that there were things more fearful even than solitude.

The stillness of the night, and the glory of the stars that had once been his friends, brought calm to the soul of Trevindor. Slowly he turned and retraced his footsteps, walking heavily, for he was about to perform a deed that no man of his kind had ever done before.

The Master was erect when Trevindor re-entered the sphere. Perhaps some hint of the other's purpose dawned upon his mind, for he was very pale. Steadfastly, Trevindor forced himself to look once more into the Master's brain. His mind recoiled at the chaos of conflicting emotions, now shot through with sickening flashes of fear. Out of the maelstrom one coherent thought came timidly quavering.

"What are you going to do? Why do you look at me like that?"

Trevindor made no reply, holding his mind aloof from contamination while he marshaled his resolution and all his strength.

The tumult in the Master's mind was rising to crescendo. For a moment his mounting terror brought something akin to pity to the gentle spirit of Trevindor, and his will faltered. But then there came again the picture of those ruined and burning cities.

With all the power of his intellect, backed by thousands of centuries of mental evolution, he struck at the man before him. Into the Master's mind, obliterating all else, flooded the single thought of—death.

For a moment the Master stood motionless, his eyes staring wildly. His breath froze as his lungs ceased their work; in his veins the pulsing blood, which had been stilled for so long, now congealed forever.

Without a sound, the Master toppled and lay still.

Very slowly Trevindor turned and walked out into the night. Like a shroud the silence and loneliness of the world descended upon him. The sand, thwarted so long, began to drift through the open portals of the Master's tomb.

Hide and Seek

We were walking back through the woods when Kingman saw the gray squirrel. Our bag was a small but varied one—three grouse, four rabbits (one, I am sorry to say, an infant in arms) and a couple of pigeons. And contrary to certain dark forecasts, both the dogs were still alive.

The squirrel saw us at the same moment. It knew that it was marked for immediate execution as a result of the damage it had done to the trees on the estate, and perhaps it had lost close relatives to Kingman's gun. In three leaps it had reached the base of the nearest tree, and vanished behind it in a flicker of gray. We saw its face once more, appearing for a moment round the edge of its shield a dozen feet from the ground; but though we waited, with guns leveled hopefully at various branches, we never saw it again.

Kingman was very thoughtful as we walked back across the lawn to the magnificent old house. He said nothing as we handed our victims to the cook—who received them without much enthusiasm—and only emerged from his reverie when we were sitting in the smoking room and he remembered his duties as a host.

"That tree-rat," he said suddenly (he always called them "tree-rats," on the grounds that people were too sentimental to shoot the dear little squirrels) "it reminded me of a very peculiar experience that happened shortly before I retired. Very shortly indeed, in fact."

"I thought it would," said Carson dryly. I gave him a glare: he'd been in the Navy and had heard Kingman's stories before, but they were still new to me.

"Of course," Kingman remarked, slightly nettled, "if you'd rather I didn't . . ."

"Do go on," I said hastily. "You've made me curious. What connection there can possibly be between a gray squirrel and the Second Jovian War I can't imagine."

Kingman seemed mollified.

"I think I'd better change some names," he said thoughtfully, "but I won't alter the places. The story begins about a million kilometers sunward of Mars. . ."

K.15 was a military intelligence operative. It gave him considerable pain when unimaginative people called him a spy, but at the moment he had much more substantial grounds for complaint. For some days now a fast enemy cruiser had been coming up astern, and though it was flattering to have the undivided attention of such a fine ship and so many highly trained men, it was an honor that K.15 would willingly have forgone.

What made the situation doubly annoying was the fact that his friends would be meeting him off Mars in about twelve hours, aboard a ship quite capable of dealing with a mere cruiser—from which you will gather that K.15 was a person of some importance. Unfortunately, the most optimistic calculation showed that the pursuers would be within accurate gun range in six hours. In some six hours five minutes, therefore, K.15 was likely to occupy an extensive and still expanding volume of space.

There might just be time for him to land on Mars, but that would be one of the worst things he could do. It would certainly annoy the aggressively neutral Martians, and the political complications would be frightful. Moreover, if his friends *had* to come down to the planet to rescue him, it would cost them more than ten kilometers a second in fuel—most of their operational reserve.

He had only one advantage, and that a very dubious one. The commander of the cruiser might guess that he was heading for a rendezvous, but he would not know how close it was or how large was the ship that was coming to meet him. If he could keep alive for only twelve hours, he would be safe. The "if" was a somewhat considerable one.

K.15 looked moodily at his charts, wondering if it was worthwhile to burn the rest of his fuel in a final dash. But a dash to where? He would be completely helpless then, and the pursuing ship might still have enough in her tanks to catch him as he flashed outward into the empty darkness, beyond all hope of rescue—passing his friends as they came sunward at a relative speed so great that they could do nothing to save him.

With some people, the shorter the expectation of life, the more sluggish are the mental processes. They seem hypnotized by the approach of death, so resigned to their fate that they do nothing to avoid it. K.15, on the other hand, found that his mind worked better in such a desperate emergency. It began to work now as it had seldom done before.

Commander Smith—the name will do as well as any other—of the cruiser *Doradus* was not unduly surprised when K.15 began to decelerate. He had half expected the spy to land on Mars, on the principle that internment was better than annihilation, but when the plotting room brought the news that the little scout ship was heading for Phobos, he felt completely baffled. The inner moon was nothing but a jumble of rock some twenty kilometers across, and not even the economical Martians had ever found any use for it. K.15 must be pretty desperate if he thought it was going to be of any greater value to him.

The tiny scout had almost come to rest when the radar operator lost it against the mass of Phobos. During the braking maneuver, K.15 had squandered most of his lead and the *Doradus* was now only minutes away—

though she was now beginning to decelerate lest she over-run him. The cruiser was scarcely three thousand kilometers from Phobos when she came to a complete halt: of K.15's ship, there was still no sign. It should be easily visible in the telescopes, but it was probably on the far side of the little moon.

It reappeared only a few minutes later, traveling under full thrust on a course directly away from the sun. It was accelerating at almost five gravities—and it had broken its radio silence. An automatic recorder was broadcasting over and over again this interesting message:

"I have landed on Phobos and am being attacked by a Z-class cruiser. Think I can hold out until you come, but hurry."

The message wasn't even in code, and it left Commander Smith a sorely puzzled man. The assumption that K.15 was still aboard the ship and that the whole thing was a ruse was just a little too naïve. But it might be a double-bluff: the message had obviously been left in plain language so that he would receive it and be duly confused. He could afford neither the time nor the fuel to chase the scout if K.15 really had landed. It was clear that reinforcements were on the way, and the sooner he left the vicinity the better. The phrase "Think I can hold out until you come" might be a piece of sheer impertinence, or it might mean that help was very near indeed.

Then K.15's ship stopped blasting. It had obviously exhausted its fuel, and was doing a little better than six kilometers a second away from the sun. K.15 *must* have landed, for his ship was now speeding helplessly out of the solar system. Commander Smith didn't like the message it was broadcasting, and guessed that it was running into the track of an approaching warship at some indefinite distance, but there was nothing to be done about that. The *Doradus* began to move toward Phobos, anxious to waste no time.

On the face of it, Commander Smith seemed the master of the situation. His ship was armed with a dozen heavy guided missiles and two turrets of electro-magnetic guns. Against him was one man in a space-suit, trapped on a moon only twenty kilometers across. It was not until Commander Smith had his first good look at Phobos, from a distance of less than a hundred kilometers, that he began to realize that, after all, K.15 might have a few cards up his sleeve.

To say that Phobos has a diameter of twenty kilometers, as the astronomy books invariably do, is highly misleading. The word "diameter" implies a degree of symmetry which Phobos most certainly lacks. Like those other lumps of cosmic slag, the asteroids, it is a shapeless mass of rock floating in space with, of course, no hint of an atmosphere and not much more gravity. It turns on its axis once every seven hours thirty-nine minutes, thus keeping the same face always to Mars—which is so close that appreciably less than half the planet is visible, the poles being below the curve of the horizon. Beyond this, there is very little more to be said about Phobos.

K.15 had no time to enjoy the beauty of the crescent world filling the sky above him. He had thrown all the equipment he could carry out of the airlock, set the controls, and jumped. As the little ship went flaming out toward the stars he watched it go with feelings he did not care to analyze. He had burned his boats with a vengeance, and he could only hope that the oncoming battleship would intercept the radio message as the empty vessel went racing by into nothingness. There was also a faint possibility that the enemy cruiser might go in pursuit, but that was rather too much to hope for.

He turned to examine his new home. The only light was the ocher radiance of Mars, since the sun was below the horizon, but that was quite sufficient for his purpose and he could see very well. He stood in the center of an irregular plain about two kilometers across, surrounded by low hills over which he could leap rather easily if he wished. There was a story he remembered reading long ago about a man who had accidentally jumped off Phobos: that wasn't quite possible—though it was on Deimos —as the escape velocity was still about ten meters a second. But unless he was careful, he might easily find himself at such a height that it would take hours to fall back to the surface—and that would be fatal. For K.15's plan was a simple one: he must remain as close to the surface of Phobos as possible—*and diametrically opposite the cruiser.* The *Doradus* could then fire all her armament against the twenty kilometers of rock, and he wouldn't even feel the concussion. There were only two serious dangers, and one of these did not worry him greatly.

To the layman, knowing nothing of the finer details of astronautics, the plan would have seemed quite suicidal. The *Doradus* was armed with the latest in ultra-scientific weapons: moreover, the twenty kilometers which separated her from her prey represented less than a second's flight at maximum speed. But Commander Smith knew better, and was already feeling rather unhappy. He realized, only too well, that of all the machines of transport man has ever invented, a cruiser of space is far and away the least maneuverable. It was a simple fact that K.15 could make half a dozen circuits of his little world while her commander was persuading the *Doradus* to make even one.

There is no need to go into technical details, but those who are still unconvinced might like to consider these elementary facts. A rocket-driven spaceship can, obviously, only accelerate along its major axis—that is, "forward." Any deviation from a straight course demands a physical turning of the ship, so that the motors can blast in another direction. Everyone knows that this is done by internal gyros or tangential steering jets, but very few people know just how long this simple maneuver takes. The average cruiser, fully fueled, has a mass of two or three thousand tons, which does not make for rapid footwork. But things are even worse than this, for it isn't the mass, but the moment of inertia that matters here—and since a cruiser is a long, thin object, its moment of inertia is slightly colossal. The sad fact remains (though it is seldom mentioned by astronautical engineers) that it takes a good ten minutes to rotate a spaceship through 180 degrees, with gyros of any reasonable

size. Control jets aren't much quicker, and in any case
their use is restricted because the rotation they produce
is permanent and they are liable to leave the ship spinning like a slow-motion pinwheel, to the annoyance of
all inside.

In the ordinary way, these disadvantages are not very
grave. One has millions of kilometers and hundreds of
hours in which to deal with such minor matters as a
change in the ship's orientation. It is definitely against
the rules to move in ten-kilometer radius circles, and
the commander of the *Doradus* felt distinctly aggrieved.
K.15 wasn't playing fair.

At the same moment that resourceful individual was
taking stock of the situation, which might very well have
been worse. He had reached the hills in three jumps and
felt less naked than he had out in the open plain. The
food and equipment he had taken from the ship he had
hidden where he hoped he could find it again, but as his
suit could keep him alive for over a day that was the
least of his worries. The small packet that was the cause
of all the trouble was still with him, in one of those
numerous hiding places a well-designed space-suit af-
fords.

There was an exhilarating loneliness about his mountain eyrie, even though he was not quite as lonely as he
would have wished. Forever fixed in his sky, Mars was
waning almost visibly as Phobos swept above the night
side of the planet. He could just make out the lights of
some of the Martian cities, gleaming pin-points marking
the junctions of the invisible canals. All else was stars and
silence and a line of jagged peaks so close it seemed he
could almost touch them. Of the *Doradus* there was still
no sign. She was presumably carrying out a careful telescopic examination of the sunlighted side of Phobos.

Mars was a very useful clock: when it was half full the
sun would rise and, very probably, so would the *Doradus*.
But she might approach from some quite unexpected
quarter: she might even—and this was the one real danger—she might even have landed a search party.

This was the first possibility that had occurred to Com-

mander Smith when he saw just what he was up against.
Then he realized that the surface area of Phobos was
over a thousand square kilometers and that he could not
spare more than ten men from his crew to make a search
of that jumbled wilderness. Also, K.15 would certainly
be armed.

Considering the weapons which the *Doradus* carried,
this last objection might seem singularly pointless. It was
very far from being so. In the ordinary course of business,
side-arms and other portable weapons are as much use
to a space-cruiser as are cutlasses and crossbows. The
Doradus happened, quite by chance—and against regu-
lations at that—to carry one automatic pistol and a hundred rounds of ammunition. Any search party would
therefore consist of a group of unarmed men looking for
a well concealed and very desperate individual who
could pick them off at his leisure. K.15 was breaking the
rules again.

The terminator of Mars was now a perfectly straight
line, and at almost the same moment the sun came up,
not so much like thunder as like a salvo of atomic bombs.
K.15 adjusted the filters of his visor and decided to move.
It was safer to stay out of the sunlight, not only because
here he was less likely to be detected in the shadow but
also because his eyes would be much more sensitive there.
He had only a pair of binoculars to help him, whereas the
Doradus would carry an electronic telescope of twenty
centimeters aperture at least.

It would be best, K.15 decided, to locate the cruiser
if he could. It might be a rash thing to do, but he would
feel much happier when he knew exactly where she was
and could watch her movements. He could then keep
just below the horizon, and the glare of the rockets would
give him ample warning of any impending move. Cautiously launching himself along an almost horizontal trajectory, he began the circumnavigation of his world.

The narrowing crescent of Mars sank below the horizon until only one vast horn reared itself enigmatically
against the stars. K.15 began to feel worried: there was
still no sign of the *Doradus*. But this was hardly surpris-

ing, for she was painted black as night and might be a good hundred kilometers away in space. He stopped, wondering if he had done the right thing after all. Then he noticed that something quite large was eclipsing the stars almost vertically overhead, and was moving swiftly even as he watched. His heart stopped for a moment: then he was himself again, analyzing the situation and trying to discover how he had made so disastrous a mistake.

It was some time before he realized that the black shadow slipping across the sky was not the cruiser at all, but something almost equally deadly. It was far smaller, and far nearer, than he had at first thought. The *Doradus* had sent her television-homing guided missiles to look tor him.

This was the second danger he had feared, and there was nothing he could do about it except to remain as inconspicuous as possible. The *Doradus* now had many eyes searching for him, but these auxiliaries had very severe limitations. They had been built to look for sunlit spaceships against a background of stars, not to search for a man hiding in a dark jungle of rock. The definition of their television systems was low, and they could only see in the forward direction.

There were rather more men on the chessboard now, and the game was a little deadlier, but his was still the advantage.

The torpedo vanished into the night sky. As it was traveling on a nearly straight course in this low gravitational field, it would soon be leaving Phobos behind, and K.15 waited for what he knew must happen. A few minutes later, he saw a brief stabbing of rocket exhausts and guessed that the projectile was swinging slowly back on its course. At almost the same moment he saw another flare far away in the opposite quarter of the sky, and wondered just how many of these infernal machines were in action. From what he knew of Z-class cruisers—which was a good deal more than he should—there were four missile-control channels, and they were probably all in use.

He was suddenly struck by an idea so brilliant that he

was quite sure it couldn't possibly work. The radio on his
suit was a tunable one, covering an unusually wide band,
and somewhere not far away the *Doradus* was pumping
out power on everything from a thousand megacycles
upward. He switched on the receiver and began to
explore.

It came in quickly—the raucous whine of a pulse transmitter not far away. He was probably only picking up a
sub-harmonic, but that was quite good enough. It D/F'ed
sharply, and for the first time K.15 allowed himself to
make long-range plans about the future. The *Doradus*
had betrayed herself: as long as she operated her missiles, he would know exactly where she was.

He moved cautiously forward toward the transmitter.
To his surprise the signal faded, then increased sharply
again. This puzzled him until he realized that he must
be moving through a diffraction zone. Its width might
have told him something useful if he had been a good
enough physicist, but he couldn't imagine what.

The *Doradus* was hanging about five kilometers above
the surface, in full sunlight. Her "non-reflecting" paint
was overdue for renewal, and K.15 could see her clearly.
As he was still in darkness, and the shadow line was
moving away from him, he decided that he was as safe
here as anywhere. He settled down comfortably so that
he could just see the cruiser and waited, feeling fairly
certain that none of the guided projectiles would come
so near the ship. By now, he calculated, the commander
of the *Doradus* must be getting pretty mad. He was perfectly correct.

After an hour, the cruiser began to heave herself round
with all the grace of a bogged hippopotamus. K.15
guessed what was happening. Commander Smith was
going to have a look at the antipodes, and was preparing
for the perilous fifty-kilometer journey. He watched very
carefully to see the orientation the ship was adopting, and
when she came to rest again was relieved to see that she
was almost broadside on to him. Then, with a series of
jerks that could not have been very enjoyable aboard, the
cruiser began to move down to the horizon. K.15 fol-

lowed her at a comfortable walking pace—if one could use the phrase—reflecting that this was a feat very few people had ever performed. He was particularly careful not to overtake her on one of his kilometer-long glides, and kept a close watch for any missiles that might be coming up astern.

It took the *Doradus* nearly an hour to cover the fifty kilometers. This, as K.15 amused himself by calculating, represented considerably less than a thousandth of her normal speed. Once she found herself going off into space at a tangent, and rather than waste time turning end over end again fired off a salvo of shells to reduce speed. But she made it at last, and K.15 settled down for another vigil, wedged between two rocks where he could just see the cruiser and he was quite sure she couldn't see him. It occurred to him that by this time Commander Smith might have grave doubts as to whether he really was on Phobos at all, and he felt like firing off a signal flare to reassure him. However, he resisted the temptation.

There would be little point in describing the events of the next ten hours, since they differed in no important detail from those that had gone before. The *Doradus* made three other moves, and K.15 stalked her with the care of a big-game hunter following the spoor of some elephantine beast. Once, when she would have led him out into full sunlight, he let her fall below the horizon until he could only just pick up her signals. But most of the time he kept her just visible, usually low down behind some convenient hill.

Once a torpedo exploded some kilometers away, and K.15 guessed that some exasperated operator had seen a shadow he didn't like—or else that a technician had forgotten to switch off a proximity fuse. Otherwise nothing happened to enliven the proceedings: in fact, the whole affair was becoming rather boring. He almost welcomed the sight of an occasional guided missile drifting inquisitively overhead, for he did not believe that they could see him if he remained motionless and in reasonable cover. If he could have stayed on the part of Phobos exactly opposite the cruiser he would have been safe even from these, he realized, since the ship would have no control there in the moon's radio-shadow. But he could think of no reliable way in which he could be sure of staying in the safety zone if the cruiser moved again.

The end came very abruptly. There was a sudden blast of steering jets, and the cruiser's main drive burst forth in all its power and splendor. In seconds the *Doradus* was shrinking sunward, free at last, thankful to leave, even in defeat, this miserable lump of rock that had so annoyingly balked her of her legitimate prey. K.15 knew what had happened, and a great sense of peace and relaxation swept over him. In the radar room of the cruiser, someone had seen an echo of disconcerting amplitude approaching with altogether excessive speed. K.15 now had only to switch on his suit beacon and to wait. He could even afford the luxury of a cigarette.

"Quite an interesting story," I said, "and I see now how it ties up with that squirrel. But it does raise one or two queries in my mind."

"Indeed?" said Rupert Kingman politely.

I always like to get to the bottom of things, and I knew that my host had played a part in the Jovian War about which he very seldom spoke. I decided to risk a long shot in the dark.

"May I ask how you happen to know so much about this unorthodox military engagement? It isn't possible, is it, that *you* were K.15?"

There was an odd sort of strangling noise from Carson. Then Kingman said, quite calmly: "No, I wasn't."

He got to his feet and went off toward the gun room.

"If you'll excuse me a moment, I'm going to have another shot at that tree-rat. Maybe I'll get him this time." Then he was gone.

Carson looked at me as if to say: "This is another house you'll never be invited to again." When our host was out of earshot he remarked in a coldly cynical voice:

"You've done it. What did you have to say that for?"

"Well, it seemed a safe guess. How else could he have known all that?"

"As a matter of fact, I believe he met K.15 after the War: they must have had an interesting conversation together. But I thought you knew that Rupert was retired from the service with only the rank of lieutenant commander. The Court of Inquiry could never see his point of view. After all, it just wasn't reasonable that the commander of the fastest ship in the Fleet couldn't catch a man in a space-suit."

Expedition to Earth

It was in the last days of the Empire. The tiny ship was far from home, and almost a hundred light-years from the great parent vessel searching through the loosely packed stars at the rim of the Milky Way. But even here it could not escape from the shadow that lay across civilization: beneath that shadow, pausing ever and again in their work to wonder how their distant homes were faring, the scientists of the Galactic Survey still labored at their never-ending task.

The ship held only three occupants, but between them they carried knowledge of many sciences, and the experience of half a lifetime in space. After the long interstellar night, the star ahead was warming their spirits as they dropped down toward its fires. A little more golden, a trifle more brilliant than the sun that now seemed a legend of their childhood. They knew from past experience that the chance of locating planets here was more than ninety per cent, and for the moment they forgot all else in the excitement of discovery.

They found the first planet within minutes of coming to rest. It was a giant, of a familiar type, too cold for protoplasmic life and probably possessing no stable surface. So they turned their search sunward, and presently were rewarded.

It was a world that made their hearts ache for home,

a world where everything was hauntingly familiar, yet never quite the same. Two great land masses floated in blue-green seas, capped by ice at either pole. There were some desert regions, but the larger part of the planet was obviously fertile. Even from this distance, the signs of vegetation were unmistakably clear.

They gazed hungrily at the expanding landscape as they fell down into the atmosphere, heading toward noon in the subtropics. The ship plummeted through cloudless skies toward a great river, checked its fall with a surge of soundless power, and came to rest among the long grasses by the water's edge.

No one moved: there was nothing to be done until the automatic instruments had finished their work. Then a bell tinkled softly and the lights on the control board flashed in a pattern of meaningful chaos. Captain Altman rose to his feet with a sigh of relief.

"We're in luck," he said. "We can go outside without protection, if the pathogenic tests are satisfactory. What did you make of the place as we came in, Bertrond?"

"Geologically stable—no active volcanoes, at least. I didn't see any trace of cities, but that proves nothing. If there's a civilization here, it may have passed that stage."

"Or not reached it yet?"

Bertrond shrugged. "Either's just as likely. It may take us some time to find out on a planet this size."

"More time than we've got," said Clindar, glancing at the communications panel that linked them to the mother ship and thence to the Galaxy's threatened heart. For a moment there was a gloomy silence. Then Clindar walked to the control board and pressed a pattern of keys with automatic skill.

With a slight jar, a section of the hull slid aside and the fourth member of the crew stepped out onto the new planet, flexing metal limbs and adjusting servo motors to the unaccustomed gravity. Inside the ship, a television screen glimmered into life, revealing a long vista of waving grasses, some trees in the middle distance, and a glimpse of the great river. Clindar punched a button, and the picture flowed steadily across the screen as the robot turned its head.

"Which way shall we go?" Clindar asked.

"Let's have a look at those trees," Altman replied. "If there's any animal life we'll find it there."

"Look!" cried Bertrond. "A bird!"

Clindar's fingers flew over the keyboard: the picture centered on the tiny speck that had suddenly appeared on the left of the screen, and expanded rapidly as the robot's telephoto lens came into action.

"You're right," he said. "Feathers—beak—well up the evolutionary ladder. This place looks promising. I'll start the camera."

The swaying motion of the picture as the robot walked forward did not distract them: they had grown accustomed to it long ago. But they had never become reconciled to this exploration by proxy when all their impulses cried out to them to leave the ship, to run through the grass and to feel the wind blowing against their faces. Yet it was too great a risk to take, even on a world that seemed as fair as this. There was always a skull hidden behind Nature's most smiling face. Wild beasts, poisonous reptiles, quagmires—death could come to the unwary explorer in a thousand disguises. And worst of all were the invisible enemies, the bacteria and viruses against which the only defense might often be a thousand light-years away.

A robot could laugh at all these dangers and even if, as sometimes happened, it encountered a beast powerful enough to destroy it—well, machines could always be replaced.

They met nothing on the walk across the grasslands. If any small animals were disturbed by the robot's passage, they kept outside its field of vision. Clindar slowed the machine as it approached the trees, and the watchers in the spaceship flinched involuntarily at the branches that appeared to slash across their eyes. The picture dimmed for a moment before the controls readjusted

themselves to the weaker illumination; then it came back
to normal.

The forest was full of life. It lurked in the under-
growth, clambered among the branches, flew through
the air. It fled chattering and gibbering through the trees
as the robot advanced. And all the while the automatic
cameras were recording the pictures that formed on the
screen, gathering material for the biologists to analyze
when the ship returned to base.

Clindar breathed a sigh of relief when the trees suddenly thinned. It was exhausting work, keeping the robot
from smashing into obstacles as it moved through the
forest, but on open ground it could take care of itself.
Then the picture trembled as if beneath a hammer-blow,
there was a grinding metallic thud, and the whole scene
swept vertiginously upward as the robot toppled and
fell.

"What's that?" cried Altman. "Did you trip?"

"No," said Clindar grimly, his fingers flying over the
keyboard. "Something attacked from the rear. I hope
. . . ah . . . I've still got control."

He brought the robot to a sitting position and swiveled
its head. It did not take long to find the cause of the
trouble. Standing a few feet away, and lashing its tail
angrily, was a large quadruped with a most ferocious set
of teeth. At the moment it was, fairly obviously, trying
to decide whether to attack again.

Slowly, the robot rose to its feet, and as it did so the
great beast crouched to spring. A smile flitted across
Clindar's face: he knew how to deal with this situation.
His thumb felt for the seldom-used key labeled "Siren."

The forest echoed with a hideous undulating scream
from the robot's concealed speaker, and the machine advanced to meet its adversary, arms flailing in front of it.
The startled beast almost fell over backward in its effort
to turn, and in seconds was gone from sight.

"Now I suppose we'll have to wait a couple of hours
until everything comes out of hiding again," said Bertrond ruefully.

"I don't know much about animal psychology," interjected Altman, "but is it usual for them to attack something completely unfamiliar?"

"Some will attack anything that moves, but that's unusual. Normally they attack only for food, or if they've already been threatened. What are you driving at? Do you suggest that there are other robots on this planet?"

"Certainly not. But our carnivorous friend may have mistaken our machine for a more edible biped. Don't you think that this opening in the jungle is rather unnatural? It could easily be a path."

"In that case," said Clindar promptly, "we'll follow it and find out. I'm tired of dodging trees, but I hope nothing jumps on us again: it's bad for my nerves."

"You were right, Altman," said Bertrond a little later. "It's certainly a path. But that doesn't mean intelligence. After all, animals—"

He stopped in mid-sentence, and at the same instant Clindar brought the advancing robot to a halt. The path had suddenly opened out into a wide clearing, almost completely occupied by a village of flimsy huts. It was ringed by a wooden palisade, obviously defense against an enemy who at the moment presented no threat. For the gates were wide open, and beyond them the inhabitants were going peacefully about their ways.

For many minutes the three explorers stared in silence at the screen. Then Clindar shivered a little and remarked: "It's uncanny. It might be our own planet, a hundred thousand years ago. I feel as if I've gone back in time."

"There's nothing weird about it," said the practical Altman. "After all, we've discovered nearly a hundred planets with our type of life on them."

"Yes," retorted Clindar. "A hundred in the whole Galaxy! I still think it's strange it had to happen to us."

"Well, it had to happen to *somebody*," said Bertrond philosophically. "Meanwhile, we must work out our contact procedure. If we send the robot into the village it will start a panic."

"That," said Altman, "is a masterly understatement. What we'll have to do is catch a native by himself and

prove that we're friendly. Hide the robot, Clindar. Somewhere in the woods where it can watch the village without being spotted. We've a week's practical anthropology
ahead of us!"

It was three days before the biological tests showed
that it would be safe to leave the ship. Even then Bertrond insisted on going alone—alone, that is, if one ig-
nored the substantial company of the robot. With such
an ally he was not afraid of this planet's larger beasts,
and his body's natural defenses could take care of the
microorganisms. So, at least, the analyzers had assured
him; and considering the complexity of the problem,
they made remarkably few mistakes. . .

He stayed outside for an hour, enjoying himself cautiously, while his companions watched with envy. It
would be another three days before they could be quite
certain that it was safe to follow Bertrond's example.
Meanwhile, they kept busy enough watching the village
through the lenses of the robot, and recording everything
they could with the cameras. They had moved the spaceship at night so that it was hidden in the depths of the
forest, for they did not wish to be discovered until they
were ready.

And all the while the news from home grew worse.
Though their remoteness here at the edge of the Universe
deadened its impact, it lay heavily on their minds and
sometimes overwhelmed them with a sense of futility. At
any moment, they knew, the signal for recall might come
as the Empire summoned up its last resources in its ex-
tremity. But until then they would continue their work as
though pure knowledge were the only thing that mattered.

Seven days after landing, they were ready to make
the experiment. They knew now what paths the villagers
used when going hunting, and Bertrond chose one of the
less frequented ways. Then he placed a chair firmly in
the middle of the path and settled down to read a book.

It was not, of course, quite as simple as that: Bertrond
had taken all imaginable precautions. Hidden in the un-
dergrowth fifty yards away, the robot was watching

through its telescopic lenses, and in its hand it held a small but deadly weapon. Controlling it from the spaceship, his fingers poised over the keyboard, Clindar waited to do what might be necessary.

That was the negative side of the plan: the positive side was more obvious. Lying at Bertrond's feet was the carcass of a small, horned animal which he hoped would be an acceptable gift to any hunter passing this way.

Two hours later the radio in his suit harness whispered a warning. Quite calmly, though the blood was pounding in his veins, Bertrond laid aside his book and looked down the trail. The savage was walking forward confidently enough, swinging a spear in his right hand. He paused for a moment when he saw Bertrond, then advanced more cautiously. He could tell that there was nothing to fear, for the stranger was slightly built and obviously unarmed.

When only twenty feet separated them, Bertrond gave a reassuring smile and rose slowly to his feet. He bent down, picked up the carcass, and carried it forward as an offering. The gesture would have been understood by any creature on any world, and it was understood here. The savage reached forward, took the animal, and threw it effortlessly over his shoulder. For an instant he stared into Bertrond's eyes with a fathomless expression; then he turned and walked back toward the village. Three times he glanced round to see if Bertrond was following, and each time Bertrond smiled and waved reassurance. The whole episode lasted little more than a minute. As the first contact between two races it was completely without drama, though not without dignity.

Bertrond did not move until the other had vanished from sight. Then he relaxed and spoke into his suit microphone.

"That was a pretty good beginning," he said jubilantly. "He wasn't in the least frightened, or even suspicious. I think he'll be back."

"It still seems too good to be true," said Altman's voice in his ear. "I should have thought he'd have been either scared or hostile. Would *you* have accepted a lavish gift from a peculiar stranger with such little fuss?"

Bertrond was slowly walking back to the ship. The robot had now come out of cover and was keeping guard a few paces behind him.

"*I* wouldn't," he replied, "but I belong to a civilized community. Complete savages may react to strangers in many different ways, according to their past experience. Suppose this tribe has never had any enemies. That's quite possible on a large but sparsely populated planet. Then we may expect curiosity, but no fear at all."

"If these people have no enemies," put in Clindar, no longer fully occupied in controlling the robot, "why have they got a stockade round the village?"

"I meant no *human* enemies," replied Bertrond. "If that's true, it simplifies our task immensely."

"Do you think he'll come back?"

"Of course. If he's as human as I think, curiosity and greed will make him return. In a couple of days we'll be bosom friends."

Looked at dispassionately, it became a fantastic routine. Every morning the robot would go hunting under Clindar's direction, until it was now the deadliest killer in the jungle. Then Bertrond would wait until Yaan—which was the nearest they could get to his name—came striding confidently along the path. He came at the same time every day, and he always came alone. They wondered about this: did he wish to keep his great discovery to himself and thus get all the credit for his hunting prowess? If so, it showed unexpected foresight and cunning.

At first Yaan had departed at once with his prize, as if afraid that the donor of such a generous gift might change his mind. Soon, however, as Bertrond had hoped, he could be induced to stay for a while by simple conjuring tricks and a display of brightly colored fabrics and crystals, in which he took a childlike delight. At last Bertrond was able to engage him in lengthy conversations, all of which were recorded as well as being filmed through the eyes of the hidden robot.

One day the philologists might be able to analyze this material; the best that Bertrond could do was to discover the meanings of a few simple verbs and nouns. This was made more difficult by the fact that Yaan not only used different words for the same thing, but sometimes the same word for different things.

Between these daily interviews, the ship traveled far, surveying the planet from the air and sometimes landing for more detailed examinations. Although several other human settlements were observed, Bertrond made no attempt to get in touch with them, for it was easy to see that they were all at much the same cultural level as Yaan's people.

It was, Bertrond often thought, a particularly bad joke on the part of Fate that one of the Galaxy's very few truly human races should have been discovered at this moment of time. Not long ago this would have been an event of supreme importance; now civilization was too hard-pressed to concern itself with these savage cousins waiting at the dawn of history.

Not until Bertrond was sure he had become part of Yaan's everyday life did he introduce him to the robot. He was showing Yaan the patterns in a kaleidoscope when Clindar brought the machine striding through the grass with its latest victim dangling across one metal arm. For the first time Yaan showed something akin to fear; but he relaxed at Bertrond's soothing words, though he continued to watch the advancing monster. It halted some distance away, and Bertrond walked forward to meet it. As he did so, the robot raised its arms and handed him the dead beast. He took it solemnly and carried it back to Yaan, staggering a little under the unaccustomed load.

Bertrond would have given a great deal to know just what Yaan was thinking as he accepted the gift. Was he trying to decide whether the robot was master or slave? Perhaps such conceptions as this were beyond his grasp: to him the robot might be merely another man, a hunter who was a friend of Bertrond.

Clindar's voice, slightly larger than life, came from the robot's speaker.

"It's astonishing how calmly he accepts us. Won't anything scare him?"

"You will keep judging him by your own standards," replied Bertrond. "Remember, his psychology is completely different, and much simpler. Now that he has confidence in me, anything that I accept won't worry him."

"I wonder if that will be true of all his race?" queried Altman. "It's hardly safe to judge by a single specimen. I want to see what happens when we send the robot into the village."

"Hello!" exclaimed Bertrond. "*That* surprised him. He's never met a person who could speak with two voices before."

"Do you think he'll guess the truth when he meets us?" said Clindar.

"No. The robot will be pure magic to him—but it won't be any more wonderful than fire and lightning and all the other forces he must already take for granted."

"Well, what's the next move?" asked Altman, a little impatiently. "Are you going to bring him to the ship, or will you go into the village first?"

Bertrond hesitated. "I'm anxious not to do too much too quickly. You know the accidents that have happened with strange races when that's been tried. I'll let him think this over, and when we get back tomorrow I'll try to persuade him to take the robot back to the village."

In the hidden ship, Clindar reactivated the robot and started it moving again. Like Altman, he was growing a little impatient of this excessive caution, but on all matters relating to alien life-forms Bertrond was the expert, and they had to obey his orders.

There were times now when he almost wished he were a robot himself, devoid of feelings or emotions, able to watch the fall of a leaf or the death agonies of a world with equal detachment. . .

The sun was low when Yaan heard the great voice crying from the jungle. He recognized it at once, despite its inhuman volume: it was the voice of his friend, and it was calling him.

In the echoing silence, the life of the village came to a stop. Even the children ceased their play: the only sound was the thin cry of a baby frightened by the sudden silence.

All eyes were upon Yaan as he walked swiftly to his hut and grasped the spear that lay beside the entrance. The stockade would soon be closed against the prowlers of the night, but he did not hesitate as he stepped out into the lengthening shadows. He was passing through the gates when once again that mighty voice summoned him, and now it held a note of urgency that came clearly across all the barriers of language and culture.

The shining giant who spoke with many voices met him a little way from the village and beckoned him to follow. There was no sign of Bertrond. They walked for almost a mile before they saw him in the distance, standing not far from the river's edge and staring out across the dark, slowly moving waters.

He turned as Yaan approached, yet for a moment seemed unaware of his presence. Then he gave a gesture of dismissal to the shining one, who withdrew into the distance.

Yaan waited. He was patient and, though he could never have expressed it in words, contented. When he was with Bertrond he felt the first intimations of that selfless, utterly irrational devotion his race would not fully achieve for many ages.

It was a strange tableau. Here at the river's brink two men were standing. One was dressed in a closely-fitting uniform equipped with tiny, intricate mechanisms. The other was wearing the skin of an animal and was carrying a flint-tipped spear. Ten thousand generations lay between them, ten thousand generations and an immeasurable gulf of space. Yet they were both human. As she must do often in eternity, Nature had repeated one of her basic patterns.

Presently Bertrond began to speak, walking to and fro in short, quick steps as he did, and in his voice there was a trace of madness.

"It's all over, Yaan. I'd hoped that with our knowledge we could have brought you out of barbarism in a dozen generations, but now you will have to fight your way up from the jungle alone, and it may take you a million years to do so. I'm sorry—there's so much we could have done. Even now I wanted to stay here, but Altman and Clindar talk of duty, and I suppose that they are right. There is little enough that we can do, but our world is calling and we must not forsake it.

"I wish you could understand me, Yaan. I wish you knew what I was saying. I'm leaving you these tools: some of them you will discover how to use, though as likely as not in a generation they'll be lost or forgotten. See how this blade cuts: it will be ages before your world can make its like. And guard this well: when you press the button—look! If you use it sparingly, it will give you light for years, though sooner or later it will die. As for these other things—find what use for them you can.

"Here come the first stars, up there in the east. Do you ever look at the stars, Yaan? I wonder how long it will be before you have discovered what they are, and I wonder what will have happened to us by then. Those stars are our homes, Yaan, and we cannot save them. Many have died already, in explosions so vast that I can imagine them no more than you. In a hundred thousand of your years, the light of those funeral pyres will reach your world and set its peoples wondering. By then, perhaps, your race will be reaching for the stars. I wish I could warn you against the mistakes we made, and which now will cost us all that we have won.

"It is well for your people, Yaan, that your world is here at the frontier of the Universe. You may escape the doom that waits for us. One day, perhaps, your ships will go searching among the stars as we have done, and they may come upon the ruins of our worlds and wonder who we were. But they will never know that we met here by this river when your race was young.

"Here come my friends; they would give me no more time. Good-by, Yaan—use well the things I have left you. They are your world's greatest treasures."

Something huge, something that glittered in the starlight, was sliding down from the sky. It did not reach the ground, but came to rest a little way above the surface, and in utter silence a rectangle of light opened in its side. The shining giant appeared out of the night and stepped through the golden door. Bertrond followed, pausing for a moment at the threshold to wave back at Yaan. Then the darkness closed behind him.

No more swiftly than smoke drifts upward from a fire, the ship lifted away. When it was so small that Yaan felt he could hold it in his hands, it seemed to blur into a long line of light slanting upward into the stars. From the empty sky a peal of thunder echoed over the sleeping land; and Yaan knew at last that the gods were gone and would never come again.

For a long time he stood by the gently moving waters, and into his soul there came a sense of loss he was never to forget and never to understand. Then, carefully and reverently, he collected together the gifts that Bertrond had left.

Under the stars, the lonely figure walked homeward across a nameless land. Behind him the river flowed softly to the sea, winding through the fertile plains on which, more than a thousand centuries ahead, Yaan's descendants would build the great city they were to call Babylon.

Loophole

From: President.
To: Secretary, Council of Scientists.

I have been informed that the inhabitants of Earth have succeeded in releasing atomic energy and have been making experiments with rocket propulsion. This is most serious. Let me have a full report immediately. And make it *brief* this time.

K.K. IV.

From: Secretary, Council of Scientists.
To: President.

The facts are as follows: Some months ago our instruments detected intense neutron emission from Earth, but an analysis of radio programs gave no explanation at the time. Three days ago a second emission occurred, and soon afterward all radio transmissions from Earth announced that atomic bombs were in use in the current war. The translators have not completed their interpretation, but it appears that the bombs are of considerable power. Two have so far been used. Some details of their construction have been released, but the elements concerned have not yet been identified. A fuller report will be forwarded as soon as possible. For the moment all that is certain is that the inhabitants of Earth *have* liberated atomic power, so far only explosively.

Very little is known concerning rocket research on Earth. Our astronomers have been observing the planet carefully ever since radio emissions were detected a generation ago. It is certain that long-range rockets of some kind are in existence on Earth, for there have been numerous references to them in recent military broadcasts. However, no serious attempt has been made to reach interplanetary space. When the war ends, it is expected that the inhabitants of the planet may carry out research in this direction. We will pay very careful attention to their broadcasts and the astronomical watch will be rigorously enforced.

From what we have inferred of the planet's technology, it should require about twenty years before Earth develops atomic rockets capable of crossing space. In view of this, it would seem that the time has come to set up a base on the Moon, so that a close scrutiny can be kept on such experiments when they commence.

                                                    Trescon.

The war on Earth has now ended, apparently owing to the intervention of the atomic bomb. This will not affect the above arguments but it may mean that the inhabitants of Earth can devote themselves to pure research again more quickly than expected. Some broadcasts have already pointed out the application of atomic power to rocket propulsion.

                                                        T.

From: President.
To: Chief of Bureau of Extra-Planetary Security. (C.B.E.P.S.)
    You have seen Trescon's minute.
    Equip an expedition to the satellite of Earth immediately. It is to keep a close watch on the planet and to report at once if rocket experiments are in progress.
    The greatest care must be taken to keep our presence on the Moon a secret. You are personally responsible

for this. Report to me at yearly intervals, or more often
if necessary.

K.K. IV.

From: President.
To: C.B.E.P.S.
  Where is the report of Earth?!!

K.K. IV.

From: C.B.E.P.S.
To: President.
  The delay is regretted. It was caused by the breakdown of the ship carrying the report.
  There have been no signs of rocket experimenting
during the past year, and no reference to it in broadcasts from the planet.

Ranthe.

From: C.B.E.P.S.
To: President.
  You will have seen my yearly reports to your re-
spected father on this subject. There have been no
developments of interest for the past fifteen years, but
the following message has just been received from our
base on the Moon:

> Rocket projectile, apparently atomically pro-
> pelled, left Earth's atmosphere today from Northern
> land-mass, traveling into space for one-quarter
> diameter of planet before returning under control.

Ranthe.

From: President.
To: Chief of State.
  Your comments, please.

K.K. V.

From: Chief of State.
To: President.
  This means the end of our traditional policy.
  The only hope of security lies in preventing the Ter-

restrials from making further advances in this direction. From what we know of them, this will require some overwhelming threat.

Since its high gravity makes it impossible for us to land on the planet, our sphere of action is restricted. The problem was discussed nearly a century ago by Anvar, and I agree with his conclusions. We must act *immediately* along those lines.

F.K.S.

From: President.
To: Secretary of State.
    Inform the Council that an emergency meeting is convened for noon tomorrow.

K.K. V.

From: President.
To: C.B.E.P.S.
    Twenty battleships should be sufficient to put Anvar's plan into operation. Fortunately there is no need to arm them—yet. Report progress of construction to me weekly.

K.K. V.

From: C.B.E.P.S.
To: President.
    Nineteen ships are now completed. The twentieth is still delayed owing to hull failure and will not be ready for at least a month.

Ranthe.

From: President.
To: C.B.E.P.S.
    Nineteen will be sufficient. I will check the operational plan with you tomorrow. Is the draft of our broadcast ready yet?

K.K. V.

From: C.B.E.P.S.
To: President.
    Draft herewith:

People of Earth!

We, the inhabitants of the planet you call Mars, have for many years observed your experiments toward achieving interplanetary travel. *These experiments must cease.* Our study of your race has convinced us that you are not fitted to leave your planet in the present state of your civilization. The ships you now see floating above your cities are capable of destroying them utterly, and will do so unless you discontinue your attempts to cross space.

We have set up an observatory on your Moon and can immediately detect any violation of these orders. If you obey them, we will not interfere with you again. Otherwise, one of your cities will be destroyed every time we observe a rocket leaving the Earth's atmosphere.

By order of the President and Council of Mars.

Ranthe.

From: President.
To: C.B.E.P.S.

I approve. The translation can go ahead.

I will not be sailing with the fleet, after all. Report to me in detail immediately on your return.

K.K. V.

From: C.B.E.P.S.
To: President.

I have the honor to report the successful completion of our mission. The voyage to Earth was uneventful: radio messages from the planet indicated that we were detected at a considerable distance and great excitement had been aroused before our arrival. The fleet was dispersed according to plan and I broadcast the ultimatum. We left immediately and no hostile weapons were brought to bear against us.

I will report in detail within two days.

Ranthe.

From: Secretary, Council of Scientists.
To: President.

The psychologists have completed their report, which is attached herewith.

As might be expected, our demands at first infuriated this stubborn and high-spirited race. The shock to their pride must have been considerable, for they believed themselves to be the only intelligent beings in the Universe.

However, within a few weeks there was a rather unexpected change in the tone of their statements. They had begun to realize that we were intercepting all their radio transmissions, and some messages have been broadcast directly to us. They state that they have agreed to ban all rocket experiments, in accordance with our wishes. This is as unexpected as it is welcome. Even if they are trying to deceive us, we are perfectly safe now that we have established the second station just outside the atmosphere. They cannot possibly develop spaceships without our seeing them or detecting their tube radiation.

The watch on Earth will be continued rigorously, as instructed.

Trescon.

From: C.B.E.P.S.
To: President.

Yes, it is quite true that there have been no further rocket experiments in the last ten years. We certainly did not expect Earth to capitulate so easily!

I agree that the existence of this race now constitutes a permanent threat to our civilization and we are making experiments along the lines you suggest. The problem is a difficult one, owing to the great size of the planet. Explosives would be out of the question, and a radioactive poison of some kind appears to offer the greatest hope of success.

Fortunately, we now have an indefinite time in which to complete this research, and I will report regularly.

Ranthe.

From: Lieutenant Commander Henry Forbes, Intelligence Branch, Special Space Corps.

To: Professor S. Maxton, Philological Department, University of Oxford.

Route: Transender II (vio Schenectady).

The above papers, with others, were found in the ruins of what is believed to be the capital Martian city. (Mars Grid KL302895.) The frequent use of the ideograph for "Earth" suggests that they may be of special interest and it is hoped that they can be translated. Other papers will be following shortly.

H. Forbes, Lt. Cmdr.

Dear Max:

Sorry I've had no time to contact you before. I'll be seeing you as soon as I get back to Earth.

Gosh! Mars *is* in a mess! Our co-ordinates were dead accurate and the bombs materialized right over their cities, just as the Mount Wilson boys predicted.

We're sending a lot of stuff back through the two small machines, but until the big transmitter is materialized we're rather restricted and, of course, none of us can return. So hurry up with it!

I'm glad we can get to work on rockets again. I may be old-fashioned, but being squirted through space at the speed of light doesn't appeal to me!

Yours in haste,

Henry.

Inheritance

As David said, when one falls on Africa from a height of two hundred and fifty kilometers, a broken ankle may be an anticlimax but it is none the less painful. But what hurt him most, he pretended, was the way we had all rushed out into the desert to see what had happened to the A.20 and hadn't come near him until hours later.

"Be logical, David," Jimmy Langford had protested. "We knew that you were O.K. because the base 'copter radioed when it picked you up. But the A.20 might have been a complete write-off."

"There's only one A.20," I said, trying to be helpful, "but rocket test-pilots are—well, if not two a penny, at any rate twelve for a dime."

David glared back at us from beneath his bushy eyebrows and said something in Welsh.

"The Druid's curse," Jimmy remarked to me. "Any moment now you'll turn into a leek or a perspex model of Stonehenge."

You see, we were still pretty light-headed and it wouldn't do to be serious for a while. Even David's iron nerve must have taken a terrific beating, yet somehow he seemed the calmest of us all. I couldn't understand it —then.

The A.20 had come down fifty kilometers from her

launching point. We'd followed her by radar for the
whole trajectory, so we knew her position to within a
few meters—though we didn't know at the time that
David had landed ten kilometers farther east.

The first warning of disaster had come seventy seconds
after takeoff. The A.20 had reached fifty kilometers and
was following the correct trajectory to within a few per
cent. As far as the eye could tell, the luminous track on the
radar screen had scarcely deviated from the pre-computed
path. David was doing two kilometers a second: not
much, but the fastest any man had ever traveled up to
then. And *Goliath* was just about to be jettisoned.

The A.20 was a two-step rocket. It had to be, for it was
using chemical fuels. The upper component, with its
tiny cabin, its folded aerofoils and flaps, weighed just
under twenty tons when fully fueled. It was to be lifted
by a lower two-hundred-ton booster which would take
it up to fifty kilometers, after which it could carry on
quite happily under its own power. The big fellow would
then drop back to Earth by parachute: it wouldn't weigh
much when its fuel was burnt. Meanwhile the upper step
would have built up enough speed to reach the six-
hundred-kilometer level before falling back and going
into a glide that would take David halfway round the
world if he wished.

I don't remember who called the two rockets *David*
and *Goliath* but the names caught on at once. Having
two Davids around caused a lot of confusion, not all of
it accidental.

Well, that was the theory, but as we watched the tiny
green spot on the screen fall away from its calculated
course, we knew that something had gone wrong. And we
guessed what it was.

At fifty kilometers the spot should have divided in
two. The brighter echo should have continued to rise as
a free projectile, and then fallen back to Earth. But the
other should have gone on, still accelerating, drawing
swiftly away from the discarded booster.

There had been no separation. The empty *Goliath* had
refused to come free and was dragging *David* back to

Earth—helplessly, for *David's* motors could not be used. Their exhausts were blocked by the machine beneath.

We saw all this in about ten seconds. We waited just long enough to calculate the new trajectory, and then we climbed into the 'copters and set off for the target area.

All we expected to find, of course, was a heap of magnesium looking as if a bulldozer had gone over it. We knew that *Goliath* couldn't eject its parachute while *David* was sitting on top of it, any more than *David* could use its motors while *Goliath* was clinging beneath. I remember wondering who was going to break the news to Mavis, and then realizing that she'd be listening to the radio and would know all about it as soon as anyone.

We could scarcely believe our eyes when we found the two rockets still coupled together, lying undamaged beneath the big parachute. There was no sign of David, but a few minutes later Base called to say that he'd been found. The plotters at Number Two Station had picked up the tiny echo from his parachute and sent a 'copter to collect him. He was in the hospital twenty minutes later, but we stayed out in the desert for several hours checking over the machines and making arrangements to retrieve them.

When at last we got back to Base, we were pleased to see our best-hated science-reporters among the mob being held at bay. We waved aside their protests and sailed on into the ward.

The shock and the subsequent relief had left us all feeling rather irresponsible and perhaps childish. Only David seemed unaffected: the fact that he'd just had one of the most miraculous escapes in human history hadn't made him turn a hair. He sat there in the bed pretending to be annoyed at our jibes until we'd calmed down.

"Well," said Jimmy at last, "what went wrong?"

"That's for you to discover," David replied. "*Goliath* went like a dream until fuel-cutoff point. I waited then for the five-second pause before the explosive bolts detonated and the springs threw it clear, but nothing happened. So I punched the emergency release. The lights

dimmed, but the kick I'd expected never came. I tried a
couple more times but somehow I knew it was useless. I
guessed that something had shorted in the detonator circuit and was earthing the power supply.

"Well, I did some rather rapid calculations from the
flight charts and abacs in the cabin. At my present speed
I'd continue to rise for another two hundred kilometers
and would reach the peak of my trajectory in about three
minutes. Then I'd start the two-hundred-and-fifty-kilo-
meter fall and should make a nice hole in the desert four
minutes later. All told, I seemed to have a good seven
minutes of life left—ignoring air-resistance, to use your
favorite phrase. That might add a couple of minutes to
my expectation of life.

"I knew that I couldn't get the big parachute out, and
David's wings would be useless with the forty-ton mass
of *Goliath* on its tail. I'd used up two of my seven minutes
before I decided what to do.

"It's a good job I made you widen that airlock. Even
so, it was a squeeze to get through it in my space-suit. I
tied the end of the safety rope to a locking lever and
crawled along the hull until I reached the junction of the
two steps.

"The parachute compartment couldn't be opened from
the outside, but I'd taken the emergency axe from the
pilot's cabin. It didn't take long to get through the magnesium skin: once it had been punctured I could almost
tear it apart with my hands. A few seconds later I'd released the 'chute. The silk floated aimlessly around me:
I had expected some trace of air-resistance at this speed
but there wasn't a sign of it. The canopy simply stayed
where it was put. I could only hope that when we re-
entered atmosphere it would spread itself without foul-
ing the rocket.

"I thought I had a fairly good chance of getting away
with it. The additional weight of *David* would increase
the loading of the parachute by less than twenty per cent,
but there was always the chance that the shrouds would
chafe against the broken metal and be worn through before I could reach Earth. In addition the canopy would

be distorted when it did open, owing to the unequal lengths of the cords. There was nothing I could do about that.

"When I'd finished, I looked about me for the first time. I couldn't see very well, for perspiration had misted over the glass of my suit. (Someone had better look into that: it can be dangerous.) I was still rising, though very slowly now. To the northeast I could see the whole of Sicily and some of the Italian mainland: farther south I could follow the Libyan coast as far as Bengasi. Spread out beneath me was all the land over which Alexander and Montgomery and Rommel had fought when I was a boy. It seemed rather surprising that anyone had ever made such a fuss about it.

"I didn't stay long: in three minutes I would be entering the atmosphere. I took a last look at the flaccid parachute, straightened some of the shrouds, and climbed back into the cabin. Then I jettisoned *David's* fuel—first the oxygen, and then, as soon as it had had time to disperse, the alcohol.

"That three minutes seemed an awfully long time. I was just over twenty-five kilometers high when I heard the first sound. It was a very high-pitched whistle, so faint that I could scarcely hear it. Glancing through the portholes, I saw that the parachute shrouds were becoming taut and the canopy was beginning to billow above me. At the same time I felt weight returning and knew that the rocket was beginning to decelerate.

"The calculation wasn't very encouraging. I'd fallen free for over two hundred kilometers and if I was to stop in time I'd need an *average* deceleration of ten gravities. The peaks might be twice that, but I'd stood fifteen g before now in a lesser cause. So I gave myself a double shot of dynocaine and uncaged the gimbals of my seat. I remember wondering whether I should let out *David's* little wings, and decided that it wouldn't help. Then I must have blacked out.

"When I came round again it was very hot, and I had normal weight. I felt very stiff and sore, and to make matters worse the cabin was oscillating violently. I struggled to the port and saw that the desert was uncomfortably close. The big parachute had done its work, but I thought that the impact was going to be rather too violent for comfort. So I jumped.

"From what you tell me I'd have done better to have stayed in the ship. But I don't suppose I can grumble."

We sat in silence for a while. Then Jimmy remarked casually:

"The accelerometer shows that you touched twenty-one gravities on the way down. Only for three seconds, though. Most of the time it was between twelve and fifteen."

David didn't seem to hear and presently I said:

"Well, we can't hold the reporters off much longer. Do you feel like seeing them?"

David hesitated.

"No," he answered. "Not now."

He read our faces and shook his head violently.

"No," he said with emphasis, "it's not that at all. I'd be willing to take off again right now. But I want to sit and think things over for a while."

His voice sank, and when he spoke again it was to show the real David behind the perpetual mask of extraversion.

"You think I haven't any nerves," he said, "and that I take risks without bothering about the consequences. Well, that isn't quite true and I'd like you to know why. I've never told anyone this, not even Mavis.

"You know I'm not superstitious," he began, a little apologetically, "but most materialists have some secret reservations, even if they won't admit them.

"Many years ago I had a peculiarly vivid dream. By itself, it wouldn't have meant much, but later I discovered that two other men had put almost identical experiences on record. One you've probably read, for the man was J. W. Dunne.

"In his first book, *An Experiment with Time*, Dunne tells how he once dreamed that he was sitting at the controls of a curious flying machine with swept-back wings, and years later the whole experience came true when he

was testing his inherent-stability aeroplane. Remembering my own dream, which I'd had *before* reading Dunne's
book, this made a considerable impression on me. But
the second incident I found even more striking.

"You've heard of Igor Sikorsky: he designed some of
the first commercial long-distance flying-boats—'Clippers,'
they were called. In his autobiography, *The Story of the
Winged-S*, he tells us how he had a dream very similar to
Dunne's.

"He was walking along a corridor with doors opening
on either side and electric lights glowing overhead.
There was a slight vibration underfoot and somehow he
knew that he was in a flying machine. Yet at that time
there were no aeroplanes in the world, and few people
believed there ever would be.

"Sikorsky's dream, like Dunne's, came true many years
later. He was on the maiden flight of his first Clipper
when he found himself walking along that familiar corridor."

David laughed, a little self-consciously.

"You've probably guessed what my dream was about,"
he continued. "Remember, it would have made no permanent impression if I hadn't come across these parallel
cases.

"I was in a small, bare room with no windows. There
were two other men with me, and we were all wearing
what I thought at the time were diving-suits. I had a
curious control panel in front of me, with a circular screen
built into it. There was a picture on the screen, but it
didn't mean anything to me and I can't recall it now,
though I've tried many times since. All I remember is
turning to the other two men and saying: 'Five minutes
to go, boys'—though I'm not sure if those were the exact
words. And then, of course, I woke up.

"That dream has haunted me ever since I became a test
pilot. No—haunted isn't the right word. It's given me
confidence that in the long run everything would be all
right—at least until I'm in that cabin with those other
two men. What happens after that I don't know. But
now you understand why I felt quite safe when I brought

down the A.20, and when I crash-landed the A.15 off
Pantelleria.

"So now you know. You can laugh if you please: I
sometimes do myself. But even if there's nothing in it,
that dream's given my subconscious a boost that's been
pretty useful."

We didn't laugh, and presently Jimmy said:

"Those other men—did you recognize them?"

David looked doubtful.

"I've never made up my mind," he answered. "Remember, they were wearing space-suits and I didn't see their
faces clearly. But one of them looked rather like you,
though he seemed a good deal older than you are now.
I'm afraid you weren't there, Arthur. Sorry."

"I'm glad to hear it," I said. "As I've told you before,
I'll have to stay behind to explain what went wrong. I'm
quite content to wait until the passenger service starts."

Jimmy rose to his feet.

"O.K., David," he said, "I'll deal with the gang outside.
Get some sleep now—with or without dreams. And by
the way, the A.20 will be ready again in a week. I think
she'll be the last of the chemical rockets: they say the
atomic drive's nearly ready for us."

We never spoke of David's dream again, but I think
it was often in our minds. Three months later he took
the A.20 up to six hundred and eighty kilometers, a
record which will never be broken by a machine of this
type, because no one will ever build a chemical rocket
again. David's uneventful landing in the Nile Valley
marked the end of an epoch.

It was three years before the A.21 was ready. She
looked very small compared with her giant predecessors,
and it was hard to believe that she was the nearest thing
to a spaceship man had yet built. This time the takeoff
was from sea level, and the Atlas Mountains which had
witnessed the start of our earlier shots were now merely
the distant background to the scene.

By now both Jimmy and I had come to share David's

belief in his own destiny. I remember Jimmy's parting words as the airlock closed.

"It won't be long now, David, before we build that three-man ship."

And I knew he was only half joking.

We saw the A.21 climb slowly into the sky in great, widening circles, unlike any rocket the world had ever known before. There was no need to worry about gravitational loss now that we had a built-in fuel supply, and David wasn't in a hurry. The machine was still traveling quite slowly when I lost sight of it and went into the plotting room.

When I got there the signal was just fading from the screen, and the detonation reached me a little later. And that was the end of David and his dreams.

The next I recall of that period is flying down the Conway Valley in Jimmy's 'copter, with Snowdon gleaming far away on our right. We had never been to David's home before and were not looking forward to this visit. But it was the least that we could do.

As the mountains drifted beneath us we talked about the suddenly darkened future and wondered what the next step would be. Apart from the shock of personal loss, we were beginning to realize how much of David's confidence we had come to share ourselves. And now that confidence had been shattered.

We wondered what Mavis would do, and discussed the boy's future. He must be fifteen now, though I hadn't seen him for several years and Jimmy had never met him at all. According to his father he was going to be an architect and already showed considerable promise.

Mavis was quite calm and collected, though she seemed much older than when I had last met her. For a while we talked about business matters and the disposal of David's estate. I'd never been an executor before, but tried to pretend that I knew all about it.

We had just started to discuss the boy when we heard the front door open and he came into the house. Mavis called to him and his footsteps came slowly along the passage. We could tell that he didn't want to meet us, and his eyes were still red when he entered the room.

I had forgotten how much like his father he was, and I heard a little gasp from Jimmy.

"Hello, David," I said.

But he didn't look at me. He was staring at Jimmy, with that puzzled expression of a man who has seen someone before but can't remember where.

And quite suddenly I knew that young David would never be an architect.

The Sentinel

The next time you see the full moon high in the south, look carefully at its right-hand edge and let your eye travel upward along the curve of the disk. Round about two o'clock you will notice a small, dark oval: anyone with normal eyesight can find it quite easily. It is the great walled plain, one of the finest on the Moon, known as the Mare Crisium—the Sea of Crises. Three hundred miles in diameter, and almost completely surrounded by a ring of magnificent mountains, it had never been explored until we entered it in the late summer of 1996.

Our expedition was a large one. We had two heavy freighters which had flown our supplies and equipment from the main lunar base in the Mare Serenitatis, five hundred miles away. There were also three small rockets which were intended for short-range transport over regions which our surface vehicles couldn't cross. Luckily, most of the Mare Crisium is very flat. There are none of the great crevasses so common and so dangerous elsewhere, and very few craters or mountains of any size. As far as we could tell, our powerful caterpillar tractors would have no difficulty in taking us wherever we wished to go.

I was geologist—or selenologist, if you want to be pedantic—in charge of the group exploring the southern region of the Mare. We had crossed a hundred miles of it in a week, skirting the foothills of the mountains along the shore of what was once the ancient sea, some thousand million years before. When life was beginning on Earth, it was already dying here. The waters were retreating down the flanks of those stupendous cliffs, retreating into the empty heart of the Moon. Over the land which we were crossing, the tideless ocean had once been half a mile deep, and now the only trace of moisture was the hoarfrost one could sometimes find in caves which the searing sunlight never penetrated.

We had begun our journey early in the slow lunar dawn, and still had almost a week of Earth-time before nightfall. Half a dozen times a day we would leave our vehicle and go outside in the space-suits to hunt for interesting minerals, or to place markers for the guidance of future travelers. It was an uneventful routine. There is nothing hazardous or even particularly exciting about lunar exploration. We could live comfortably for a month in our pressurized tractors, and if we ran into trouble we could always radio for help and sit tight until one of the spaceships came to our rescue.

I said just now that there was nothing exciting about lunar exploration, but of course that isn't true. One could never grow tired of those incredible mountains, so much more rugged than the gentle hills of Earth. We never knew, as we rounded the capes and promontories of that vanished sea, what new splendors would be revealed to us. The whole southern curve of the Mare Crisium is a vast delta where a score of rivers once found their way into the ocean, fed perhaps by the torrential rains that must have lashed the mountains in the brief volcanic age when the Moon was young. Each of these ancient valleys was an invitation, challenging us to climb into the unknown uplands beyond. But we had a hundred miles still to cover, and could only look longingly at the heights which others must scale.

We kept Earth-time aboard the tractor, and precisely at 22.00 hours the final radio message would be sent out to Base and we would close down for the day. Outside, the rocks would still be burning beneath the almost vertical sun, but to us it was night until we awoke again eight hours later. Then one of us would prepare breakfast, there would be a great buzzing of electric razors, and someone would switch on the short-wave radio from Earth. Indeed, when the smell of frying sausages began to fill the cabin, it was sometimes hard to believe that we were not back on our own world—everything was so normal and homely, apart from the feeling of decreased weight and the unnatural slowness with which objects fell.

It was my turn to prepare breakfast in the corner of the main cabin that served as a galley. I can remember that moment quite vividly after all these years, for the radio had just played one of my favorite melodies, the old Welsh air, "David of the White Rock." Our driver was already outside in his space-suit, inspecting our caterpillar treads. My assistant, Louis Garnett, was up forward in the control position, making some belated entries in yesterday's log.

As I stood by the frying pan waiting, like any terrestrial housewife, for the sausages to brown, I let my gaze wander idly over the mountain walls which covered the whole of the southern horizon, marching out of sight to east and west below the curve of the Moon. They seemed only a mile or two from the tractor, but I knew that the nearest was twenty miles away. On the Moon, of course, there is no loss of detail with distance—none of that almost imperceptible haziness which softens and sometimes transfigures all far-off things on Earth.

Those mountains were ten thousand feet high, and they climbed steeply out of the plain as if ages ago some subterranean eruption had smashed them skyward through the molten crust. The base of even the nearest was hidden from sight by the steeply curving surface of the plain, for the Moon is a very little world, and from where I was standing the horizon was only two miles away.

I lifted my eyes toward the peaks which no man had ever climbed, the peaks which, before the coming of

terrestrial life, had watched the retreating oceans sink
sullenly into their graves, taking with them the hope and
the morning promise of a world. The sunlight was beating against those ramparts with a glare that hurt the eyes,
yet only a little way above them the stars were shining
steadily in a sky blacker than a winter midnight on Earth.

I was turning away when my eye caught a metallic
glitter high on the ridge of a great promontory thrust-
ing out into the sea thirty miles to the west. It was a di-
mensionless point of light, as if a star had been clawed
from the sky by one of those cruel peaks, and I imagined
that some smooth rock surface was catching the sunlight
and heliographing it straight into my eyes. Such things
were not uncommon. When the Moon is in her second
quarter, observers on Earth can sometimes see the great
ranges in the Oceanus Procellarum burning with a blue-
white iridescence as the sunlight flashes from their slopes
and leaps again from world to world. But I was curious
to know what kind of rock could be shining so brightly
up there, and I climbed into the observation turret and
swung our four-inch telescope round to the west.

I could see just enough to tantalize me. Clear and
sharp in the field of vision, the mountain peaks seemed
only half a mile away, but whatever was catching the
sunlight was still too small to be resolved. Yet it seemed
to have an elusive symmetry, and the summit upon which
it rested was curiously flat. I stared for a long time at that
glittering enigma, straining my eyes into space, until
presently a smell of burning from the galley told me that
our breakfast sausages had made their quarter-million
mile journey in vain.

All that morning we argued our way across the Mare
Crisium while the western mountains reared higher in
the sky. Even when we were out prospecting in the space-
suits, the discussion would continue over the radio. It
was absolutely certain, my companions argued, that there
had never been any form of intelligent life on the Moon.
The only living things that had ever existed there were a
few primitive plants and their slightly less degenerate
ancestors. I knew that as well as anyone, but there are

times when a scientist must not be afraid to make a fool of himself.

"Listen," I said at last, "I'm going up there, if only for my own peace of mind. That mountain's less than twelve thousand feet high—that's only two thousand under Earth gravity—and I can make the trip in twenty hours at the outside. I've always wanted to go up into those hills, anyway, and this gives me an excellent excuse."

"If you don't break your neck," said Garnett, "you'll be the laughing-stock of the expedition when we get back to Base. That mountain will probably be called Wilson's Folly from now on."

"I won't break my neck," I said firmly. "Who was the first man to climb Pico and Helicon?"

"But weren't you rather younger in those days?" asked Louis gently.

"That," I said with great dignity, "is as good a reason as any for going."

We went to bed early that night, after driving the tractor to within half a mile of the promontory. Garnett was coming with me in the morning; he was a good climber, and had often been with me on such exploits before. Our driver was only too glad to be left in charge of the machine.

At first sight, those cliffs seemed completely unscaleable, but to anyone with a good head for heights, climbing is easy on a world where all weights are only a sixth of their normal value. The real danger in lunar mountaineering lies in overconfidence; a six-hundred-foot drop on the Moon can kill you just as thoroughly as a hundred-foot fall on Earth.

We made our first halt on a wide ledge about four thousand feet above the plain. Climbing had not been very difficult, but my limbs were stiff with the unaccustomed effort, and I was glad of the rest. We could still see the tractor as a tiny metal insect far down at the foot of the cliff, and we reported our progress to the driver before starting on the next ascent.

Inside our suits it was comfortably cool, for the refrigeration units were fighting the fierce sun and carrying

away the body-heat of our exertions. We seldom spoke
to each other, except to pass climbing instructions and
to discuss our best plan of ascent. I do not know what
Garnett was thinking, probably that this was the craziest
goose-chase he had ever embarked upon. I more than half
agreed with him, but the joy of climbing, the knowledge
that no man had ever gone this way before and the exhilaration of the steadily widening landscape gave me
all the reward I needed.

I don't think I was particularly excited when I saw in
front of us the wall of rock I had first inspected through
the telescope from thirty miles away. It would level off
about fifty feet above our heads, and there on the plateau
would be the thing that had lured me over these barren
wastes. It was, almost certainly, nothing more than a
boulder splintered ages ago by a falling meteor, and with
its cleavage planes still fresh and bright in this incorrupt-
ible, unchanging silence.

There were no hand-holds on the rock face, and we
had to use a grapnel. My tired arms semed to gain new
strength as I swung the three-pronged metal anchor
round my head and sent it sailing up toward the stars.
The first time it broke loose and came falling slowly back
when we pulled the rope. On the third attempt, the
prongs gripped firmly and our combined weights could
not shift it.

Garnett looked at me anxiously. I could tell that he
wanted to go first, but I smiled back at him through the
glass of my helmet and shook my head. Slowly, taking
my time, I began the final ascent.

Even with my space-suit, I weighed only forty pounds
here, so I pulled myself up hand over hand without
bothering to use my feet. At the rim I paused and waved
to my companion, then I scrambled over the edge and
stood upright, staring ahead of me.

You must understand that until this very moment I
had been almost completely convinced that there could
be nothing strange or unusual for me to find here. Almost, but not quite; it was that haunting doubt that had

driven me forward. Well, it was a doubt no longer, but
the haunting had scarcely begun.

I was standing on a plateau perhaps a hundred feet
across. It had once been smooth—too smooth to be natural—but falling meteors had pitted and scored its surface through immeasurable eons. It had been leveled
to support a glittering, roughly pyramidal structure, twice
as high as a man, that was set in the rock like a gigantic,
many-faceted jewel.

Probably no emotion at all filled my mind in those first
few seconds. Then I felt a great lifting of my heart, and a
strange, inexpressible joy. For I loved the Moon, and now
I knew that the creeping moss of Aristarchus and Eratos-
thenes was not the only life she had brought forth in her
youth. The old, discredited dream of the first explorers
was true. There had, after all, been a lunar civilization—
and I was the first to find it. That I had come perhaps a
hundred million years too late did not distress me; it was
enough to have come at all.

My mind was beginning to function normally, to analyze and to ask questions. Was this a building, a shrine—
or something for which my language had no name? If a
building, then why was it erected in so uniquely inaccessible a spot? I wondered if it might be a temple, and
I could picture the adepts of some strange priesthood
calling on their gods to preserve them as the life of the
Moon ebbed with the dying oceans, and calling on their
gods in vain.

I took a dozen steps forward to examine the thing more
closely, but some sense of caution kept me from going
too near. I knew a little of archaeology, and tried to guess
the cultural level of the civilization that must have
smoothed this mountain and raised the glittering mirror
surfaces that still dazzled my eyes.

The Egyptians could have done it, I thought, if their
workmen had possessed whatever strange materials these
far more ancient architects had used. Because of the
thing's smallness, it did not occur to me that I might be
looking at the handiwork of a race more advanced than
my own. The idea that the Moon had possessed intelli-

gence at all was still almost too tremendous to grasp,
and my pride would not let me take the final, humiliating
plunge.

And then I noticed something that set the scalp
crawling at the back of my neck—something so trivial
and so innocent that many would never have noticed it
at all. I have said that the plateau was scarred by
meteors; it was also coated inches-deep with the cosmic
dust that is always filtering down upon the surface of
any world where there are no winds to disturb it. Yet
the dust and the meteor scratches ended quite abruptly
in a wide circle enclosing the little pyramid, as though an
invisible wall was protecting it from the ravages of time
and the slow but ceaseless bombardment from space.

There was someone shouting in my earphones, and I
realized that Garnett had been calling me for some time.
I walked unsteadily to the edge of the cliff and signaled
him to join me, not trusting myself to speak. Then I went
back toward that circle in the dust. I picked up a frag-
ment of splintered rock and tossed it gently toward the
shining enigma. If the pebble had vanished at that invisible barrier I should not have been surprised, but it
seemed to hit a smooth, hemispherical surface and slide
gently to the ground.

I knew then that I was looking at nothing that could
be matched in the antiquity of my own race. This was
not a building, but a machine, protecting itself with
forces that had challenged Eternity. Those forces, whatever they might be, were still operating, and perhaps I
had already come too close. I thought of all the radiations
man had trapped and tamed in the past century. For all
I knew, I might be as irrevocably doomed as if I had
stepped into the deadly, silent aura of an unshielded
atomic pile.

I remember turning then toward Garnett, who had
joined me and was now standing motionless at my side.
He seemed quite oblivious to me, so I did not disturb him
but walked to the edge of the cliff in an effort to marshal
my thoughts. There below me lay the Mare Crisium—
Sea of Crises, indeed—strange and weird to most men,

but reassuringly familiar to me. I lifted my eyes toward the crescent Earth, lying in her cradle of stars, and I wondered what her clouds had covered when these unknown builders had finished their work. Was it the steaming jungle of the Carboniferous, the bleak shoreline over which the first amphibians must crawl to conquer the land —or, earlier still, the long loneliness before the coming of life?

Do not ask me why I did not guess the truth sooner— the truth that seems so obvious now. In the first excitement of my discovery, I had assumed without question that this crystalline apparition had been built by some race belonging to the Moon's remote past, but suddenly, and with overwhelming force, the belief came to me that it was as alien to the Moon as I myself.

In twenty years we had found no trace of life but a few degenerate plants. No lunar civilization, whatever its doom, could have left but a single token of its existence.

I looked at the shining pyramid again, and the more remote it seemed from anything that had to do with the Moon. And suddenly I felt myself shaking with a foolish, hysterical laughter, brought on by excitement and overexertion: for I had imagined that the little pyramid was speaking to me and was saying: "Sorry, I'm a stranger here myself."

It has taken us twenty years to crack that invisible shield and to reach the machine inside those crystal walls. What we could not understand, we broke at last with the savage might of atomic power and now I have seen the fragments of the lovely, glittering thing I found up there on the mountain.

They are meaningless. The mechanisms—if indeed they are mechanisms—of the pyramid belong to a technology that lies far beyond our horizon, perhaps to the technology of para-physical forces.

The mystery haunts us all the more now that the other planets have been reached and we know that only Earth has ever been the home of intelligent life in our Universe. Nor could any lost civilization of our own world have built that machine, for the thickness of the meteoric dust on the plateau has enabled us to measure its age. It was set there upon its mountain before life had emerged from the seas of Earth.

When our world was half its present age, *something* from the stars swept through the Solar System, left this token of its passage, and went again upon its way. Until we destroyed it, that machine was still fulfilling the purpose of its builders; and as to that purpose, here is my guess.

Nearly a hundred thousand million stars are turning in the circle of the Milky Way, and long ago other races on the worlds of other suns must have scaled and passed the heights that we have reached. Think of such civilizations, far back in time against the fading afterglow of Creation, masters of a universe so young that life as yet had come only to a handful of worlds. Theirs would have been a loneliness we cannot imagine, the loneliness of gods looking out across infinity and finding none to share their thoughts.

They must have searched the star-clusters as we have searched the planets. Everywhere there would be worlds, but they would be empty or peopled with crawling, mindless things. Such was our own Earth, the smoke of the great volcanoes still staining the skies, when that first ship of the peoples of the dawn came sliding in from the abyss beyond Pluto. It passed the frozen outer worlds, knowing that life could play no part in their destinies. It came to rest among the inner planets, warming themselves around the fire of the Sun and waiting for their stories to begin.

Those wanderers must have looked on Earth, circling safely in the narrow zone between fire and ice, and must have guessed that it was the favorite of the Sun's children. Here, in the distant future, would be intelligence; but there were countless stars before them still, and they might never come this way again.

So they left a sentinel, one of millions they have scattered throughout the Universe, watching over all worlds with the promise of life. It was a beacon that down the ages has been patiently signaling the fact that no one had discovered it.

Perhaps you understand now why that crystal pyramid was set upon the Moon instead of on the Earth. Its builders were not concerned with races still struggling up from savagery. They would be interested in our civilization only if we proved our fitness to survive—by crossing space and so escaping from the Earth, our cradle. That is the challenge that all intelligent races must meet, sooner or later. It is a double challenge, for it depends in turn upon the conquest of atomic energy and the last choice between life and death.

Once we had passed that crisis, it was only a matter of time before we found the pyramid and forced it open. Now its signals have ceased, and those whose duty it is will be turning their minds upon Earth. Perhaps they wish to help our infant civilization. But they must be very, very old, and the old are often insanely jealous of the young.

I can never look now at the Milky Way without wondering from which of those banked clouds of stars the emissaries are coming. If you will pardon so commonplace a simile, we have set off the fire-alarm and have nothing to do but to wait.

I do not think we will have to wait for long.

About Arthur C. Clarke

IN A recent issue, *Holiday* magazine acclaimed Arthur C. Clarke as "the colossus of science fiction"—and with good reason. He has already completed a body of works, both in fiction and non-fiction, which has clearly established his reputation as a careful scientist and a superbly gifted writer of imaginative literature. THE EXPLORATION OF SPACE, his non-fiction book on the coming age of interplanetary flight, was a Book-of-the-Month Club choice. *The Atlantic Monthly* praised it as "an exceptionally lucid job of scientific exposition for the layman." His novel CHILDHOOD'S END, a breathtaking speculation on the future evolution of man, was hailed by *The New York Times* as "a first rate tour de force that is well worth the attention of every thoughtful citizen in this age of anxiety."

A fellow of the Royal Astronomical Society and former Chairman of the British Interplanetary Society, Arthur C. Clarke brings the discipline and the intellectual horizons of science to the service of a truly original and powerful imagination. The result is fiction of the future with an unusual relevance for our times. (His story "Superiority," for example, is required reading at the Massachusetts Institute of Technology.)

Mr. Clarke's interest in science began early. "When I was less than ten years old," he writes, "I built a small telescope from a cardboard tube and a couple of lenses, and spent many of my nights mapping the moon, until I knew my way around it a good deal better than around my native Somerset.

"The science-fiction virus attacked me when I was fourteen and saw my first copies of *Amazing Stories* and *Astounding*. For years I collected every issue I could lay my hands upon; I can still recall the thrill of receiving an entire crateful of *Wonder Stories* which I'd purchased for five cents apiece.

"When I was around fifteen I started writing short pieces for the school magazine and eventually became its assistant editor. On turning up these articles recently, I was depressed to see how little improvement there had been in the interim.

"Moving to London I encountered the British science-fiction world as well as the embryo British Interplanetary Society. Was treasurer of the B.I.S., edited, wrote for, and duplicated countless science-fiction 'fan mags,' and sold my first articles on space flight.

"The War and the R.A.F. introduced me to radar. The experience I gained running the first Ground-Controlled Approach equipment has been reflected in a number of my stories and has given me an insight into the scientific mind.

"With the help of a friendly Member of Parliament I obtained our equivalent of a G.I. scholarship to Kings College, London, and passed out two years later with a First Class Honors B.Sc. in physics and pure and applied math.

"Meanwhile I had started selling stories to the science-fiction magazines in the United States. I continued writing fiction and nonfiction after I'd left college and became Assistant Editor of Physics Abstracts—a very interesting job that kept me in touch with scientific progress. Threw this up after two years when my spare-time income began to exceed my salary.

"In 1950 my first book was published—a technical work called *Interplanetary Flight*, which was so successful despite its specialized nature that I was asked to do a second book for the general public. This was *The Exploration of Space*.

In the mid-50's, however, my career took a new direction when I was badly bitten by the skin-diving virus. (I have since infected other astronauts, notably Dr. Wernher von Braun.) In 1955 I joined my partner Mike Wilson on the Great Barrier Reef of Australia, with results reported in *The Coast of Coral*. Later expeditions took us to Ceylon, where we have now made our home. Mike's discovery of the first treasure ship ever found in the Indian Ocean (a heavily-armed trader that went down in 1702 carrying at least a ton of silver coins) resulted in the book and TV movie "The Treasure of the Great Reef," and plunged our lives into a confusion from which we have not yet extricated ourselves.

At the moment I am approaching my fortieth book, and would probably have reached it by now if not for a three-year detour with Stanley Kubrick, writing the novel and screenplay of "2001: A Space Odyssey." Having long ago abandoned hope of catching up with Isaac Asimov's output, I have now restricted myself to a couple of minor ambitions:—

I *intend* to go to the Moon when the tourist service starts; and I *hope* (but hardly expect) to go to Mars. . . .

Arthur C. Clarke
Colombo, November 1966

BY ARTHUR C. CLARKE
IN BALLANTINE BOOKS EDITIONS

In Science Fiction
Ballantine Books Brings You
the Best of the Established Authors
and the Most Exciting New Writers

፠፠፠፠፠፠፠፠፠፠፠፠፠፠፠፠፠፠፠፠፠፠፠፠፠

WORLD OF PTAVVS	Larry Niven	60¢
NEUTRON STAR	Larry Niven	75¢
FAHRENHEIT 451	Ray Bradbury	60¢
TARNSMAN OF GOR	John Norman	75¢
OUTLAW OF GOR	John Norman	75¢
TO OPEN THE SKY	Robert Silverberg	75¢
THORNS	Robert Silverberg	75¢
THE MASKS OF TIME	Robert Silverberg	75¢
CHOCKY	John Wyndham	75¢
RESTOREE	Anne McCaffrey	75¢
DRAGONFLIGHT	Anne McCaffrey	75¢
CHTHON	Piers Anthony	75¢
THE WORM OUROBOROS	E. R. Eddison	95¢
MISTRESS OF MISTRESSES	E. R. Eddison	95¢
A FISH DINNER IN MEMISON	E. R. Eddison	95¢
TITUS GROAN ⎫	Mervyn Peake	95¢
GORMENGHAST ⎬ Trilogy	Mervyn Peake	95¢
TITUS ALONE ⎭	Mervyn Peake	95¢
DOLPHIN BOY	Roy Meyers	75¢
DAUGHTERS OF THE DOLPHIN		
	Roy Meyers	75¢

◆